VWK
VAMPIRE WARRIOR KINGS

HE'S HER DARKEST FANTASY...

In the Service of the KING

NEW YORK TIMES BESTSELLER
LAURA KAYE

In the Service of the KING

VWK
VAMPIRE WARRIOR KINGS

NEW YORK TIMES BESTSELLER
LAURA KAYE

IN THE SERVICE OF THE KING

SECOND EDITION March 2020

FIRST EDITION February 2012

IN THE SERVICE OF THE KING © Laura Kaye.

ALL RIGHTS RESERVED.

No part or whole of this book may be used, reproduced, distributed, or transmitted in any manner whatsoever without written permission of the author except in the case of brief quotations embodied in critical articles or reviews. The unauthorized reproduction or distribution of this copyrighted work via electronic or mechanical means is a violation of international copyright law and subjects the violator to severe fines and/or imprisonment. If you are reading the ebook, it is licensed for your personal enjoyment only. The ebook may not be re-sold or given away to other people. If you would like to share the ebook, please purchase an additional copy for each person you share it with. Please do not participate in piracy of copyrighted materials in violation of the author's rights. Thank you for respecting the author's work.

The characters and events portrayed in this book are fictional and/or are used fictitiously and are solely the product of the author's imagination. Any similarity to persons living or dead, places, businesses, events, or locales is purely coincidental.

Cover Design by Kim Killion

THE VAMPIRE WARRIOR KINGS SERIES

IN THE SERVICE OF THE KING
SEDUCED BY THE VAMPIRE KING
TAKEN BY THE VAMPIRE KING

CHAPTER 1

VWK

Kael paced the length of his private sleeping chamber, avoiding the plush emerald carpet and keeping to the uncovered stone floor at the edge of the room. After an hour of ceaseless movement, the cold of the large polished slabs bit into the flesh of his bare feet and gave him something to focus on besides the Proffering, which he loathed but required. Three months had passed since his last feeding, and the Warrior King needed the blood of either his mate or a human virgin to maintain his immortality and the strength of his humanity.

He had no mate, and no intention of acquiring one.

But Kael the Fair never felt less like his name than when he stepped into his feeding chamber and found the Proffered waiting within.

"My lord? It is time." Liam's deep voice sounded from the hallway.

Kael halted before the wide carved mahogany door, his layered dark green and navy tartan robes settling around him. He rolled his shoulders and tilted his head to the side to stretch his neck. The familiar weight of the intricate jeweled braid on the left side of his head moved as he tried to release the tension seizing his muscles. The jewels were the most obvious of the physical marks of his royal rank; the rest were written into his skin.

Tonight, of all nights, he felt the burden of the duty and obligation they represented.

"My lord?" Liam pushed the door open and stepped back.

Kael sliced his fangs into his tongue to keep from snapping at the man who had stood at his side for the past seven hundred years. Equally ancient and nearly physically matched, Liam was the brother Kael never had and knew the king as well as any living being could. On many occasions they had stood together against their enemy, the Soul Eaters, so named not just for draining the blood of their human victims, but for consuming their souls as well by drinking through the last stutter of their hearts. Then removing and eating it.

All vampires required human blood, but only the Soul Eaters gave in to the lure of exsanguination, became addicted to the kill, and murdered their human prey. And their selfish and increasingly brazen actions were making it harder to hide their collective existence from the mass of humanity.

Kael and Liam didn't speak as they navigated the worn stone corridors of the king's ancestral estate. The underground compound was located far beneath the ancient walls of Castle Dunluce, within the craggy cliffs on the coast of County Antrim in Northern Ireland. Kael's clan, the MacQuillans, had inhabited the land since the late sixteenth century and transformed a small existing tower house into a sprawling, indomitable fortification meant to provide Kael and his vampire brethren the privacy and security they required.

In modern times, Kael chose to dispel unauthorized prying of the aboveground ruins by turning over their management to Northern Ireland as a state historic site. The arrangement provided maintenance to the castle remains and landscape during the problematic daylight hours, dedicated security, and humans loyal to the MacQuillan "descendants" who visited the site occasionally and supported its preservation with large, regular bequests. It was rather like hiding in plain sight.

The normally busy halls of the castle's central manor house were empty, as Kael preferred on the Night of the Proffering, and only dimly lit by occasional wooden torches. The compound possessed every modern convenience and security mechanism, but firelight comforted the Warrior King, and put him in mind of times of old, before the conflict with the Soul Eaters had become so constant and tiresome.

On the castle's walls, medieval tapestries hung next to Renaissance portraiture and modern art, but Kael gave his priceless collections little regard. He wanted the strength that feeding provided, but hated the means by which it had to be obtained. To be sure, the Proffering sustained him. He required it. But it also reminded him of all he'd lost, and what he'd never have again.

Finally and too quickly, they arrived at the antechamber to the set of apartments used by the Proffered when on the grounds. Liam opened the door and stood back, bowing his head of shoulder-length brown hair—braided at the left in the way of the warrior, and allowed the king to enter ahead of him. "After you, my lord."

Kael stepped into the oval room and huffed. "Would you cut the 'my lord' crap already?" He rolled his neck again. As a room, it wasn't particularly remarkable—it was bare except for a small altar at one end and hooks for his robes and a few ceremonial implements at the other. But it was so loaded with everyone's expectations that the air felt thick as he drew it down his throat.

Liam grinned before schooling his expression. "As you wish, my lord."

Kael growled and rolled his eyes, knowing even as he'd uttered the words Liam wouldn't heed them. Fat lot of good being king was sometimes. But Liam was too steeped in the traditions of their people. He often treated Kael just as one of the warriors—which only a handful of the warriors were comfortable doing—but not on the Night of the Proffering.

Tonight, to Liam, he was Kael the Fair, Warrior King of the Vampires, Chieftain of Clan MacQuillan.

Like it or not, Kael had a role to play for his people, obligations to his men, and needs that required fulfillment. Out of tradition and deference, once the Night of the Proffering was scheduled, the rest of the clan warriors would not feed until their king had his sustenance, so despite Kael's desire to put this night off—and his ability to go punishing stretches without feeding—he was acutely aware that denying himself meant denying his men. And the war with the Soul Eaters required well-blooded warriors. So Kael fed even when he might have gone without, and Liam's adherence to the traditions helped him remember the significance of the night.

It was bigger than his needs, his desires, his fears.

A familiar clattering sound drew Kael from his thoughts. He turned to find Liam on his knees, carefully covering the jade dais with hundreds of small, faceted emeralds. The stones looked nearly black in the low light of the single torch, but Kael could see their exact vivid shade of green in his mind's eye. The emerald was the sacred stone of his people, representing life and renewal. Liam recited an old Celtic prayer to the spirits of the Chieftains as he worked, then he swiftly backed away and cleared the altar for the king's sacrifice.

With purpose, Kael stepped up to the dais, opened his robes, and knelt onto the jewel-encrusted altar. The traditional pose required his knees, shins and the tops of his feet be flush against the surface, and that he sit back but not relax his bottom against his heels. He had to hold the position for ninety-three minutes—one minute for each day since his last feeding—but his massive thighs never quivered for an instant, never once belied the strain his muscles endured as they settled his six-and-a-half-foot frame in a semi-seated position.

Crimson and emerald mixed together on the platform almost immediately as the king's blood dripped out of the dozens of cuts and punctures the jewels inflicted as a sacrifice on his lower legs. Liam stepped up behind him and removed the robes.

Kael centered his mind and concentrated, easily tuning out the quiet sounds Liam made as he crossed the room to hang the garments. Later, after the Warrior King entered the feeding chamber, Liam would collect the bloodied stones into an ancient glass urn for display in the Hall of the Chieftains—the ceremonial center of the compound. The urn's contents reaffirmed the ancient belief, "life gives blood gives life," and its appearance in the hall signaled the warriors they could feed.

Kael chanted these ancient words in his head, words of life, bonds, sacrifice, honor. His focus was absolute—neither pain nor apprehension nor Liam's efficient movements around the room distracted him from the precision of his position and prayer.

Instinctively, he knew when he'd served his sacrifice. He blinked open his eyes, which strained a little against the flickering yellow light. Liam was long gone, but he'd readied everything Kael needed, as he always did.

Carefully, the king rose to his feet, stepped off the jeweled dais and gently removed the stones that were embedded in his flesh, then returned them to rest with the others. He retrieved the cloth laid out on the edge of the altar and wiped the blood from his wounds. He healed quickly and cared little about the injuries, but there was no sense scaring the Proffered with unnecessary gore.

She was probably already nervous enough.

His skin cleaned, Kael picked up the leather knife holster and strapped it to his thigh. The dagger it held was lean and vicious, but used correctly offered a quick and nearly painless cut that saved the Proffered from the piercing of his fangs into her soft flesh. Or, perhaps more accurately, the knife saved him from learning whether the woman could be his mate. Only by fully joining his body with the Proffered—by feeding directly from her veins as his cock took her virginity, could he determine if she had the potential to walk beside him as his partner in leadership, life, and love.

But Kael didn't want to know. Kael didn't want a mate. He'd had one.

Meara and their newling son had died in childbirth following the stress of an attack by the Soul Eaters on Dunluce, the very attack that brought ruin to the castle and drove them to expand the existing underground apartments into a full-out compound. While Kael and his men had eradicated that fiercest and most troublemaking band of Soul Eaters of the eighteenth century, his clan's losses had been great. Ever since, Kael had vowed never to chance again the lives of those he loved. Given the dire state of the war in recent years, that meant never chancing love again.

Yet, Kael's very biology yearned to seek out the mate connection so strongly it was nearly painful—his fangs throbbed in search of the satisfying pressure of teeth slicing mated flesh. His balls clenched for the release of his unrealized progeny. His chest tightened against the centuries-old loneliness.

Still, he held fast, wanting to protect himself, the Proffered, and her family. He would take only what he had to from her, and no more.

He wouldn't take her affection. He wouldn't take her humanity. He wouldn't risk her life.

No matter how much she or his people might want—no matter how much, in those dark, nearly forgotten corners of his mind, *he* might want—he wouldn't fall in love.

So the dagger was necessary. He'd soothe the Proffered using his hypnotic words and eyes, then bleed her into a goblet before sealing her wound with a quick swipe of his tongue—the closest he allowed himself to drinking from her, and then, only out of necessity. As the blood from the goblet infused his system, his ancient chemistry would allow him to do no other than slake his body's primal thirst for carnal connection with the woman in front of him. But there would be no biting, no feeding directly from her vein and, therefore, no chancing the mate connection.

The Proffered were specially groomed for this role by human families around the world in alliance with the vampires. The seven surviving vampire kings, related by ancient kinship ties or blood rites, each ruled over a region of the world. Together, they coordinated their offensive campaigns against the Soul Eaters.

Over the years, one strategy they'd developed was the careful cultivation of influential human allies, known collectively as the Electorate. The Electorate was committed to keeping the secret of the vampires' existence, helped divert human attention from the war, and increasingly assisted militarily in the war itself. They also provided the Proffered as potential mates—required because a vampire could only be born and not made, and all vampires newlings were male.

In return, the vampire kings repaid them with their protection and their blood, which cured disease and slowed the aging process significantly. The Electorate understood that mating their human daughters with the kings and their warriors would enshrine the Vampire-Electorate Alliance for all time, cementing a partnership through familial relations that otherwise existed through diplomacy alone.

But, as with Kael, the war had left many of his vampire

brethren hesitant to develop emotional ties that could be used against them.

Without mates, fewer newlings were born every year.

Knife holster in place, Kael walked to the hooks at the rear of the room and retrieved the innermost robe—a dark green silk that skimmed over his weary body and billowed behind him as he walked. He tied the belt around his waist in a careless knot and approached the feeding chamber.

Taking a deep, centering breath, the king eased the heavy wooden door open and stepped inside.

Kael pierced his tongue with his fangs to keep from making an utterance he had no business making. But for the love of all that was holy, the woman before him was magnificent.

Perfectly posed despite the thundering sprint of her heart, her long black-brown hair was braided and intertwined in the traditional way, ribbons and flowers threaded throughout. The sheerest of white silk robes did little to hide from his vision the sexy muscularity of her body. She was not thin, which pleased him. He had once turned away a Proffered for being too thin—he was 250 pounds and nearly feral once blooded, and he'd feared crushing her. Instead, this woman appeared strong, athletic. She was young, to be sure, but also womanly, with curves where women should have curves, with rounded flesh that would have filled his exploring hands and strong grip.

Were he to allow himself the pleasure. Which he damn well wouldn't.

He stepped before her kneeling, submissive form and swallowed the blood his fangs had drawn into his mouth. "Tell me, young one, what is your name?"

CHAPTER 2

After years of imagining this very moment, he was speaking to her. And, oh, God, what a voice. Deep, resonating and slightly accented, it dragged over her like a caress.

Oh, he asked me something…what did he ask? Her brain engaged again and her lips fell open. "Shayla, Your Highness, Shayla McKinnon."

"It is a pleasure to meet you, Shayla. I am Kael, Son of Iain, Warrior King of the Vampires, Chieftain of Clan MacQuillan."

His introduction set her insides to trembling.

Vampire.

At one time, the concept had been impossible to conceive. But she'd been forced to confront the reality of their existence one cold winter night when men in uniforms and dark suits had arrived at her family's home and delivered the news her older sister had been murdered. At fourteen, Shayla had been completely devastated. Though she realized her father's position as editor-in-chief of a major

Irish newspaper made him a prominent figure in their community, she'd known nothing of her parents' high-level role in the Electorate Council.

Hadn't known it existed at all.

But once she found out, knowledge was power, and the only thing that provided any solace to her grief was learning there were other vampires, good vampires, who fought the vile creatures who had harmed Dana.

From that moment on, purpose and a sense of mission filled Shayla's life. She vowed to find a way to join that fight, a role she could fill in advance of inheriting her parents' positions on the Electorate Council upon their deaths. So, when the offer to become one of the Proffered arrived, she jumped at the chance. If she could do nothing else, sustaining the warriors battling evil would make a contribution, if small.

But she wanted to do more.

A restlessness to help fueled her, driving her to overload classes and take summer school such that she graduated high school before her sixteenth birthday. She began university and the Proffered training in tandem, completing the latter at nineteen, readying her to perform her duties for one of the vampires some time during her twentieth year. College graduation occurred soon after.

Her interest in this Warrior King had even ignited an academic curiosity about Celtic history and culture, and she'd built on her training by pursuing those studies at the graduate level. Imagining what he'd seen in his long lifetime and what she could learn from him inspired her interest in the medieval history of the British Isles, now so central to the intellectual identity she'd developed for herself.

IN THE SERVICE OF THE KING

Toward what end she did all this, she didn't quite know, but it felt right. And the fire in her gut demanded action, cried for vengeance.

The king padded across the mostly bare floor, circling her. The weight of his observation settled over her. She girded her muscles to brace against the tremors she almost couldn't help. "Do you know why you are here?" he asked as he stopped before her once more.

Shayla inhaled to speak, but froze. *You're going to have to try harder than that.* She mentally high-fived herself for not making such an elementary slip. He hadn't specifically told her to respond, now, had he?

Excitement and adrenaline made her stomach flip-flop. How Shayla had hoped this man, this vampire king, would live up to her years of fantasizing. Once she'd learned, during her Proffered training, of his incredible exploits against the Soul Eaters—and his losses—the idea of meeting him, *serving* him, had quieted her restlessness like nothing before. She'd busted her butt working to the top of the class of Profferds, earning the notice and mentorship of the most experienced and connected trainer. All for the chance of serving Kael the Fair, a chance she was so very thrilled to have this night.

Just being in his presence was a dream come true, and she determined to face her duty with strength and courage no matter what else happened. Though, the thought he would need her, might find her attractive, desirable even, was such an incredible turn-on she'd had no problem protecting her virtue from her few suitors over the years. So, her innocence was his to take, if he would have it.

She felt no shame in that.

She only wished he would want her time and time again, but knew that wasn't his practice.

Shayla frowned and internally chided herself for letting her thoughts run away with her. If she wasn't careful, she would make a mistake. She inhaled a deep, cleansing breath and cleared her mind, assessed her position. She held the pose just as she'd been taught: knees on the floor and spread, bottom resting on her heels, back and shoulders erect, hands resting on her thighs palms up, head down, eyes diverted. Her submission was part of her offering; it communicated the voluntary nature of her presence before the Warrior King.

As she knelt there, the thin white silk robe the only barrier between his blazing eyes and her flesh, she'd never felt more brave, more in control of herself…more alive.

She drew strength from those feelings and awaited the king's command.

Kael smiled down at the top of her head, and felt a little like testing her. He didn't practice domination with all of his sexual partners, though the challenges inherent in it thrilled his intellect and his libido. But, given how tightly he had to control himself in order to restrain his natural instincts when in the presence of the Proffered, he'd long ago realized restricting their behavior, words, and actions would enable his own control.

"You may answer my question, Shayla. Do you know why you are here?"

A light pink bloomed on her pale cheeks. "I am here to offer myself in whatever capacity might please you, Sire."

The king tilted his head as his gaze raked over her, absorbing every detail of her appearance, observing every quiet shift in her downcast expression. "Indeed," Kael murmured. He reached down and stroked her dark hair, which was silky and fine. When she unleashed a little gasp, he made a fist to resist his urge to plunge his hand into the beautiful mass of hair.

Finally, he resumed his pacing until he came round to stand in front of her again. "Look at me."

She responded immediately to the direct command, tilting her head back but keeping her expression passive. That didn't stop him from noticing the dilation of her eyes as they settled on him.

He sucked in a breath.

He would've been impressed with her responsiveness if he hadn't been so completely enthralled by those eyes. Her left iris was a brilliant emerald, nearly rivaling his own in the intensity and clarity of green. Her right, however, was a bright turquoise, touched by green to be sure, but without question a deep, dazzling blue. The effect of her mismatched gaze, paired as it was with her fair, creamy skin and dark tresses, was arresting. His mouth gaped in rapture of her beauty.

Powerless to resist, he leaned down and cupped her left cheek in his hand. He stroked his thumb across her cheekbone, his finger playing with the ends of her eyelashes. "You have been touched by magic."

Her breathing stuttered and her eyes grew glassy. She blinked the threatening tears away. "Thank you, Your

Majesty," she whispered. She pressed her face into his hand, just the tiniest bit.

That one small movement seemed weighted with emotion and affection, drawing Kael into personal conversation he rarely offered the Proffered. "Am I to understand that tonight actually marks your birthday?"

Shayla bit her lip and nodded.

The image of her teeth buried in plump flesh made his body tighten. Her birthday, how wonderfully unusual. It happened, of course, though the Proffered's blood was most potent any time during her twentieth year. "Well, Shayla McKinnon, I will try to make it a good one for you, yes?"

Her smile was warm, glorious. "Thank you, Sire."

The way she looked at him sent ripples of electricity through his blood. His fangs elongated. Kael pressed his lips together and dropped his hand, backing away.

Something like confusion shadowed her face before she straightened her expression and lowered her gaze once more.

Those eyes are going to be a problem.

He was drawn to them, to her. He wanted to pull her up from the floor and onto the bed, and lay her out on her side as he rested facing her. He wanted to learn about her as he stared into those magical eyes. And he *never* wanted to learn about any of the Proffered. He never allowed himself to imagine them as companions.

He was on dangerous ground.

But her face was like a mask of his people's mythology. One eye offered the green of their sacred stone, and the other the hue they cherished for its representation of fidelity, loyalty. Her porcelain skin reflected the purity of intent the diamond in his hair stood for, and her dark red lips were the color of life-giving blood. Her face was a mirror of the sacred stones—emerald, sapphire, diamond, ruby—hanging in his hair.

It had to…mean something. Didn't it?

No!

He hadn't realized he'd growled in response to his thoughts until Shayla jumped. Kael resumed his earlier pacing, growing more frustrated at himself and the situation as he thought about the dangerous impossibility of his emerging desires for her. He was half tempted to send her away, but he couldn't bring himself to do it. And that turned his frustration into anger.

He marched to the large cabinet in the corner and wrenched open the doors. The left one banged against the wall and ricocheted back at him. He yanked out a drawer and drew a heavy black eye mask from among the items displayed within. He had to hide those eyes.

He stalked across the room and stopped just behind Shayla's now-trembling form. Remarkably, he noted in passing admiration, it was the first fear she'd demonstrated since he'd walked into the room….

He shook his head. "Rise, Proffered."

Shayla complied immediately, but was as confused by his suddenly harsh tone as by him calling her by her title rather than her name. She'd been warned he might do so, but he'd been using her name so freely just moments before.

Not only that, but his declaration—*you have been touched by magic*—had been so affectionate and earnest it filled her heart with the acceptance and appreciation of her appearance she hadn't always found growing up. Kids had teased her about her "mutant eyes," and it wasn't until adulthood that she'd come to prize their uniqueness and ignore the mean comments and staring gazes. The admiring tone in his words had fueled the secret hope she harbored that tonight would lead to something more, something meaningful.

Blackness cut off her thoughts. Cool fabric covered her eyes and she swayed at the unexpected loss of her vision. His large hands on her shoulders steadied and inflamed her, and she immediately regretted the loss of their heat when he drew them away.

"Hold out your left arm." His voice held none of the warmth of before, none of the soothing welcoming tone that had calmed and reassured her earlier.

She followed the command, reining in her rising disappointment as she did so. How stupid of her to read anything into his kindness. She'd been warned what would occur this night—and what wouldn't. And yet, she'd allowed her imagination to run away with her, and she'd formed impossible expectations.

"Come." Kael supported her arm and led her across the room. She resisted gripping onto his wrist, despite the instincts that implored her otherwise, and soon she was following his command to sit.

The chair was hard and forced her into the straightest posture. Kael arranged her arm on the wide downward-slanting surface of the armrest. Her wrist and hand hung off the end. Knowing what was coming, Shayla's heart rate spiked and her breathing became shallow.

Something threaded between her arm and side, and warmth grazed her left breast. She barely restrained a gasp. A stretchy band bit into her bicep over the silk of her robe. None of this was unexpected, though she had thought she would have the use of her eyes to watch him work. She took a deep breath and forced her shoulders to relax.

Focusing on her memory of his appearance helped. God, she'd barely been able to breathe when she'd first laid eyes on him. He was…the most fascinating man she had ever seen. The vibrant deep green of his eyes was surreal. Dim lighting seemed to reflect out of them and, like an animal's eyes, they glowed and flashed. His amazing mane of bronze hair hung down over his shoulders, and a braid with green, red, blue and clear stones tied back the hair on one side of his head, revealing the incredible angularity of his masculine face. His brow was strong, pronounced, and his cheekbones were high and sharp. His square jaw framed a mouth so full and expressive her own mouth filled with saliva at the thought of getting to taste him. Lust and desire had barreled through her veins, making his mood change all the more disorienting.

No matter. What *she* wanted wasn't their purpose. A cold wetness washed over her wrist before being wiped away. What mattered most was what *he* needed—to maintain his strength in the war against the Soul Eaters. And she was willing to give. It was why she was here.

Kael needed to get this over with. Shayla's—no, the *Proffered's*—presence seemed to be sucking the very air out of the room and, with it, his control. There was just something about her. He needed this to be over and for her to be gone.

That would fix everything.

He rushed through his preparations, not taking the usual time to reassure the Proffered, to ease her fear. He appreciated the sacrifices they made for his well-being, and so his normal practice was to take every precaution to limit their fear, reduce their pain. Now, he did the minimum, drawing solace from her poise and calmness. She didn't seem to need the same bolstering as some of the other Proffereds. He admired her for that.

Which was the problem in a nutshell.

Kael pulled the wooden stand holding the ceremonial goblet in front of the corner of the Proffered's chair and positioned it to catch the blood that would flow from her wrist.

"Listen to my voice," he began.

Normally, he would've used his eyes too, the combination of voice and eyes being the most effective at completing the hypnotism, but he just…couldn't.

"I wish to have your blood. You will not feel pain, and I will make it so you bear no lasting injury. Do not be frightened. I wish you only to feel pleasure in giving me this most sacred of gifts and to know how much I appreciate your offering." Kael rushed through the words and felt a little odd he couldn't see his assurances reflected back in her expression.

He removed the blade from its holster.

"Do you give your blood freely, Proffered?" The knife hovered over her wrist.

She didn't answer, and he glanced from her wrist to her face.

He hadn't given her permission to answer. Such discipline, despite the stressed scent of her adrenaline in the air. Just who was testing whom here? "Answer me."

"Yes, Your Highness, I give you my blood freely. It's yours." Her voice was clear, firm.

He had no idea what possessed her to add on that final declaration, but he had no business liking the sentiment as much as he did. An odd tingling skittered over his right hand and his cock stirred under his robe. He shook off the rising fog of arousal. He had to do this. Now.

Kael drew the dagger across the soft unblemished skin of her wrist. A red ribbon bloomed immediately, along with the rich, spicy aroma of her lifeblood, and Kael placed the knife on the edge of the stand next to the golden goblet.

"Beautiful," he whispered. He glanced at her face. Her cheeks had paled, but otherwise she was silent, still. Her heart sounded out the same staccato beat as before. "You are doing so well, Proffered. Be at ease."

As crimson droplets pooled in the deep cup, Kael reached up and released the tourniquet, increasing the fragrant flow. He swallowed thickly, his body anticipating, responding. Desire set his muscles on edge.

The cup filled steadily, perfectly. Kael inhaled and the heady scent of her offering collided with every nerve in his body. He gasped and his mouth dropped open. Though he wouldn't need them, his fangs elongated further and demanded he taste the thick warm liquid, quench his endless thirst. Ancient instincts whispered dark promises in his ear and urged him to claim her, skin to skin, mouth to throat. His erection roared to life at his imaginings and pushed easily against the thin silk of his robe.

Nearly panting, he licked his bottom lip repeatedly. Had he ever felt such hunger?

When he glanced up at Shay...er, the Proffered's face, her bottom lip was quivering.

Kael frowned as his mind raced and unease settled like a rock in his gut.

Though the cup was not quite filled, he bent immediately and licked his healing saliva across her wound. The exquisite flavor of her lifeblood exploded inside his mouth and his cock twitched and wept.

A single tear rolled out from under the right side of her eye blindfold.

Kael's loins deflated as he sucked in a breath. Dread slid like ice down his spine. He reached out and eased the mask up and off her eyes. The strap on one side tangled in a braid and pulled it loose. A white flower fluttered down into her lap.

Her eyes, so beautiful, so expressive, told him how badly he'd messed up.

What have I done?

CHAPTER 3

Shayla couldn't meet his eyes.

If she did, she knew the tear she'd been unable to restrain would turn into the first of many. The relief of his tongue's caress had just been so beautifully complete, easing her after the slicing cut of the blade had ignited a conflagration up her whole arm.

She hadn't really believed the bloodletting would be fully painless—how could someone make a knife wound painless, after all? But she also hadn't expected it to hurt quite so bad. She'd been worried she wouldn't be able to hold out against the stinging pain, that her weakness would disappoint him. When it was finally over, she'd lost control, just for a moment. She was so pissed at herself for crying in front of the king.

"You must tell me—" The king's voice was tense, words clipped. "—did you feel the blade?" Dark energy rolled off him like a storm. The hair on her arms and neck raised and prickled.

Not meeting his gaze, she nodded once.

"Say it."

Shayla inhaled a deep breath. "Yes, Your Highness, I felt the blade."

He shot to his feet and held his hands out from his body, imploringly. "And you did not think to say so? You must have known from your training that wasn't...right."

She shook her head and shrugged her shoulders. His disappointment in her was like a punch to the gut.

"Answer me!" His voice reverberated around the stone room.

Her gaze turned to his. It was the first time she'd violated her submissive role, meeting his eyes without permission, but his anger stirred up hers. "I endured it for you. I did not wish to displease you, but it appears I have done so anyway. So, I'm sorry I have not lived up to your expectations, but I didn't know what else to do." She held his gaze, annoyed that she found him so damn sexy even though she was angry.

None of this was her fault. Was it? No.

Preternatural light reflected out from behind the emerald of his eyes. She could only describe his expression as bewildered, and his loss of control, even if only in hiding his reaction, softened her anger. Finally, when she could take his intense observation no longer, she dropped her gaze back into her lap.

Could this night go any worse?

She thought about what remained to happen between them and sagged against the unyielding wood of her seat.

Oh, God. Yes, there was every chance this night could get worse.

Please, God and any other deity listening, don't let me disappoint the ancient sex god vampire warrior king in bed.

Kael threw his hands in the air and growled.

The sound startled Shayla but it also stirred a tingling sensation low in her belly. In another situation, his feral outburst, so full of power and otherworldliness, would have been entirely arousing. He paced again, and though she knew by his clenched jaw and fists he was angry, she was almost amused at what she assumed was a nervous habit. Head still down, she watched him from beneath her eyelashes. The movement of his lithe body mesmerized her.

⁂

Kael's chest clenched and his stomach soured with his guilt over harming her. His weakness had driven him to cover her eyes, led him to rush through his normal preparations, kept him from assuring the needs of the Proferred—caused him to hurt her. His voice should've been enough, had been enough with others, but somehow he wasn't surprised to find something else distinctive about this woman.

About Shayla.

Not in three hundred years had he failed someone this egregiously. The comparison to Meara was so unexpected, he faltered in his step. Not since her had a Proffered twisted him up inside so badly. What was going on with him tonight?

He chanced a sideways glance at the beautiful source of his turmoil.

Over his seven centuries of life, many blades had pierced

his skin. He knew the awful burn of sharp metal against unprotected flesh. Yet, she'd sat there so silent, so stoic.

To have done that...God, her strength.

Not to mention the way she'd defended herself. When was the last time someone had addressed him so forthrightly, had dared to express anger at him? Well, Liam did occasionally, but few others. Her actions put her in rather elite company.

And she was right. None of this was her fault. It was his, all his. He should send her away, now, before he made things worse.

He stopped pacing and faced her. The chair forced her into an erect posture, causing her breasts to thrust forward against the robe. Her dark nipples visibly pressed into the thin fabric. Kael's fangs ached to bite into the mounded flesh of her ample breasts. He saw himself in his mind's eye: striding across the room, falling to his knees between her parted thighs, pulling the gauzy material apart and devouring her slowly but surely....

The exact opposite of what his own best judgment told him to do.

As his eyes raked over this imagined scene, they fell on the goblet still perched under her hanging left wrist. The smell of precious lifeblood hung thick in the air. He salivated. Primal need demanded he have it, *now.* The urge was almost magnetic, cosmic.

But the way it had been obtained...

As he debated, Shayla drew her shoulders back, exaggerating her posture, as if she was girding herself for something. Her fingers fluttered for a moment before gripping the arms of the chair. She shook her head. Finally, she drew a breath. "May I speak, Your Highness?"

The steadiness of Shayla's voice intrigued him. Once again, she surprised him, and yet her approach in initiating a conversation fell entirely within her role. Strong, disciplined, magical, sensual, beautiful...her appealing attributes multiplied with each passing minute.

Wary, Kael nodded. "Speak freely."

Her body eased forward on the wooden seat, setting off alarm bells in Kael's head. Almost in slow motion, Shayla sank to her knees in front of the chair and assumed the waiting position in every manner except one: rather than rest her hands palm up on her thighs, she reached with her left hand and grasped the goblet, then cupped it in between both hands and held it above her head, up to him.

"If it pleases you, Your Highness."

Kael's heartbeat stuttered, then took off at a sprint. Her initiative was daring and so damn sexy his groin tightened in anticipation. He unthinkingly added courageousness to her growing résumé. And fuck if the dramatic gaping of her robe wasn't the most decadent thing he'd ever seen. The top of the silk opened in a plunging V that revealed the rounded, heaving flesh of her breasts. But it was the bottom of the robe that exposed previously hidden territory. As she'd slid to the ground, her knees had pulled the hem back, and her open-kneed pose gave him a direct view of the dark triangle of hair between her strong, shapely thighs.

The sweetness of her body's natural lubricant combined with the rich, thirst-quenching promise of her dark offering proved an overwhelming aphrodisiac, spoke to parts of his soul he thought long dormant. Blood pounded through his head. His fangs throbbed. His cock jerked..

"Aw, hell," he muttered as his instincts took over and cast his thinking consciousness into a dark corner. He stalked up to her and pulled the goblet from her hand, then placed it back on the stand. His hands threaded under her arms and, with little effort, pulled her to her feet.

Holding her lovely face, he pressed his mouth to hers.

Shayla's mind erupted into a cacophony of joyous confusion. She'd been specifically told there would be no kissing. The king did not kiss.

But, *holy hell!* Did the king ever kiss.

His large frame bent down over her, surrounding her in his heat. His full lips sucked and pulled at hers and his tongue demanded entrance and exploration, which she freely granted. His hard muscles bunched and thrummed around her, setting her body on fire everywhere they touched. The scent of powerful masculinity filled her nose, and the exquisite flavor of his tongue in her mouth intoxicated her. And, oh God, every time she felt the passing hardness of his fangs as they kissed made her whimper and moan. Her body readied itself immediately for his, moistening, opening.

Having shielded herself from physical relationships, she was astounded to learn her body had the ability to produce this crazy, urgent euphoria. Her brain scrambled to process each new, maddening sensation. In that moment, she would've done anything to maintain the feeling.

IN THE SERVICE OF THE KING

Was it always like this?

Kael growled low in his chest as his mouth came at her again and again, and Shayla felt the vibration of the feral sound against her breasts. She squeezed her thighs together, seeking friction to satisfy even a little of her now uncontrollable lust. Her mouth was so filled with his probing tongue it was difficult to get enough oxygen, but his kisses convinced her she could live without it as long as he continued to devour her so intensely.

Never had she imagined the expression of physical love could make her feel so wanted, so needed.

His obvious pleasure throbbed against her stomach and flooded her with unbelievable feelings of power, and just a little fear. Because they were off the grid now, outside the bounds of the rules and expectations she'd been taught during her training. And she was thrilled it might mean he was as affected by her as she was by him. Wherever the king was leading them, she was only too happy to follow. In truth, she felt powerless to do otherwise.

A sharp, piercing sensation nicked the edge of her tongue. She gasped into his mouth. *He bit me! They said he wouldn't—*

All thinking abruptly halted as he sucked on her tongue and fed.

The intense suction made her knees go weak and her core clench. She sagged against his chest and threw her arms under his and up around his broad back so she could grasp onto his shoulders for leverage. The suction pulled through her tongue again and again, lighting up her entire nervous system and promising to make her come if it continued. She dug her nails into his bunching muscles as he rocked his thick cock against her belly. She pushed up onto tiptoe to bring her aching, wet center closer to where she knew instinctively they both needed it. He gripped her tighter as he bent his knees and rolled his hips against her lower pelvis, teasing her by inching ever so much nearer her aching clit. She could hardly tolerate the pressure building inside her. He sucked and sucked at her until the overwhelming pleasure of it all sent her into a dizzying and explosive orgasm unlike any she had ever had by herself.

A long, high-pitched moan ripped up her throat.

Her legs lost all feeling and she fell against him entirely as all the muscles in the center of her body pulsed and clenched. His hands flew down to catch her weight and he pulled back from the kiss for the first time in what seemed like hours—glorious, ecstatic hours.

Trembling shudders rippled through her body over and over. The waves of sensation trapped her, lifted her up and spun her around. Finally, her muscles quieted. Sheer amazement and a deep, warm satiation flooded through her blood.

Struggling to focus, she smiled up at the king.

Kael's expression visibly chilled in the moments after she met his gaze. He shook her lightly and pushed her back from his body. "Stand."

Shayla stumbled one step then caught herself, but her mind was still flying just enough she couldn't fully make sense of his actions. "Sire?"

"No." He shook his head and wiped at his mouth. His fists clenched and unclenched, and then he shook out his hands like they ached.

Shayla's stomach plummeted to the floor. Her equilibrium faltered and she stumbled another step as the room seemed to bend and twist.

The king stalked to the door in the back corner through which she had entered and hammered two swift blows with his fist against the wooden surface. "Retrieve the Proffered."

"What? No!" Shayla didn't know whether to be pissed at the king's mixed signals or mortified at his apparent displeasure in kissing her, in bringing her to orgasm.

But what she didn't want to know was his rejection. Not when he was her best hope for quenching the vengeful fire burning in her gut. But, more than that, the girlish dream that she could find a connection with someone as magnificent and mysterious and powerful as Kael the Fair didn't seem so childish anymore. Not after what she'd experienced tonight. She might be inexperienced, but she knew what she felt, and she hadn't imagined it. Some sort of primal, magnetic pull existed between them. She felt it in her bones, in her blood. Her heart squeezed and thrummed in recognition of the odd, compelling sensation.

She had to make him believe in it, too. She resumed her submissive standing pose and lowered her head. "I will do better, Your Highness, please."

"Leave." He paced from the back door toward the ornate one through which he had entered.

Her whole body trembled at the impossible direction of their conversation. "No. Please. We can still—"

"Go. Now!" His words roared and echoed through the stone chamber.

Shayla jumped. Her tears flowed unbidden and she turned to retreat. Her first shaky step knocked her into the stand on which the goblet of her own blood still sat. The cup bobbled threateningly, a splash of crimson spilling out and staining a line of dark red against the bright white of her robe, before she caught and righted it. The sight of the crimson stain brought a whimper from her tightening throat and set her into a flat out run to the door.

She hadn't seen it open, but her trainer stood there, face etched with disappointment and confusion, waiting to escort her away from the chamber, away from the Warrior King of the Vampires.

CHAPTER 4

"**D**amnaigh sé go léir don diabhal!" Kael's damning curse roared through the empty chamber.

Fucking hell, he'd lost his goddamned mind. Lost all control. Fed from her.

The knick of his fang against her sweet tongue hadn't been intentional, at least he didn't think so, but once he'd tasted her luscious blood, there was no going back. Each pull had warmed his chest, flooded him with power, and reverberated directly to his cock, driving him to get in her in his desire. He'd imagined the tight velvet clenching of her pussy around every inch of his length, unleashing the urge to thrust against her, seek out her wet entrance. Her allure was like a siren spinning dark promises in the night. Promises of paradise in the slick heat of her womanhood.

Promises that, just maybe, forever existed in the cradle of her thighs.

And then she had come. If he'd thought her beautiful before, it was nothing compared to her magnificence at the peak of ecstasy.

But as he watched her ride out her high, his mind came back to him in starts and stops.

He'd kissed her. She'd embraced him. He'd *drunk* from her. And he'd been about to fuck her standing right there in the center of the room as he devoured her lifeblood down his throat.

And to top it all off, his hands fucking tingled.

No. *No.*

Kael paced and tugged at his hair, spitting out a stream of expletives and plaintive pleas for guidance and assistance in his native tongue. "Cén bhrí atá ann? Cad é cuspóir an Céilí Dia ann?" If only the gods would answer him and explain his purpose—and why he felt so lonely fulfilling it.

Ancient grief joined the raging river flowing through him and filled him with the need to destroy. He glared at the offending goblet of Shayla's blood, but couldn't bring himself to waste something so precious. Instead, Kael whirled, nearly upsetting a long mahogany console table, and unthinkingly cleared it in one violent swipe of his arms. Candlesticks and a vase of flowers clanged and crashed against the floor.

The ornate door exploded open and a trio of massive bodies filled the entryway, guns and blades drawn.

"My lord?" Liam rasped, his eyes wild as he surveyed the room. Braeden and Daire followed suit, braced for a fight.

Kael shared a blood connection with the highest-ranking warriors that gave them the ability to sense his emotions, so he wasn't particularly surprised by their appearance, though the last thing he wanted was an audience for his stupidity.

He glared at the bewildered men. The scene was almost comical. Liam, still in his full regalia associated with the feeding ritual, Braeden and Daire dressed only in boxing shorts, their taped fists revealing they'd come directly from a sparring match in the compound's massive training facility.

"Jesus, smell that," Daire whispered to Braeden as he lowered his weapon.

Kael leveled his narrowed gaze at the young warrior. Braeden placed a warning hand on his mouthy brethren's chest.

Liam watched the exchange and turned to his men. "All is well. Leave us."

Braeden bowed his head and stepped back through the door first. "Come on, Daire," he bit out.

Daire inhaled deeply, taking the myriad scents still so thick and fragrant in the room into himself. Finally realizing everyone was waiting for him, he shook his head, bowed it and retreated.

Liam secured the door before nailing Kael with a questioning stare.

The king turned away and resumed pacing and ranting under his breath.

"My lord, how may I be of service?" came Liam's voice after a while.

"You can leave."

"I cannot."

Kael flashed in front of him. "You can very well fucking leave." His fangs elongated as he lashed out.

"I will not!" Liam stepped forward, apparently refusing to be cowed. "You really want to do this?"

They hadn't come to blows in ages, but it had happened before. The king bored his gaze into Liam's, but finally stepped back.

Liam eased his stance. "Where is she?"

"Gone," Kael said as he looked down at the ground. His shoulders sagged as some of the fight went out of him. Everything just felt so...wrong.

"Did you—?"

Kael rolled his eyes at Liam. There was no way he didn't smell that goblet of blood. "What do you think?"

"And, why—?"

"Christ, what are you? The Inquisition?" He drilled his angry stare into his brother in arms. Guilt flooded him. Minutes passed. "I hurt her." He shook his hands where they hung by his sides, the phantom tingle still racing through his nerves.

Liam tracked those movements, his brow cranked down low, and frowned. "What happened, Kael?"

The thought of recounting all the ways in which he'd failed Shayla exhausted him. "It doesn't matter."

"That's bullshit and you know it." Liam sheathed the silver dagger and holstered his weapon. "I've known you my whole life. You would never hurt a female. Not intentionally."

"What do you want from me, Liam?"

He held out his arms. "I want to know why you sent her away. Why her lifeblood sits there wasting. Why you are more distressed than I can remember seeing you in aeons."

"Oh, for the love... Fine. Her eyes were mismatched... one green, one blue. I covered them, because they were too damned fascinating. And then the hypnotism didn't work. And she felt the cut of my blade, endured it without complaint. And I...I didn't even fucking notice her pain. Then, as if she hadn't proven herself worthy, she implored me to partake of her blood anyway, despite the way I'd failed her. I kissed her, Liam. And I drank from her. And then…"

It had felt so damn right.

But now she was gone. Her absence weighed on his shoulders, depressing him, squeezing his chest. Oh, the way he'd dismissed her… He groaned and scrubbed at his face with rough palms.

Liam gaped at Kael's rush of words. "You drank from her?"

"Did I not just say that?"

"Kael, did you claim her? Is she—?"

His heart clenched. "Of course I didn't. I cannot." He met Liam's questioning gaze. Held it for a long moment. Tried like hell to resist the dark realizations fighting to rise up from his psyche, demanding to be embraced, believed, voice.

Kael swallowed roughly as a war waged inside him—between duty and desire, rightness and need, decision and destiny. He shook his head against the growing urge inside him to hope, to try, to be brave enough to take a chance.

"Liam," he finally whispered, "I did not have to claim her. Somehow, I could…I could tell…" He shook his head again.

Liam sucked in a breath and his eyes went wide.

Though the righteousness of the admission nearly drove him to his knees, Kael still resisted the truth of it. He sighed, a sound full of defeat and resignation. "As I said, it does not matter. She's gone. And it is better for her that she is."

"Do not be a fool, brother."

"Watch your tongue, Liam."

The warrior ran his hand through his brown hair, then stalked close until he grasped Kael's shoulder. "Don't assume you know what's best for her. Bring her back. Let her choose." Kael dropped his gaze, unable to witness the hope on his brother's face a moment longer. "You must, Kael, you cannot continue this way."

Kael shoved the hand away and stepped back. "I do not see you seeking out a mate. Or most of the others."

Liam scoffed. "I have not found her. But I *look*. As for the others, *you* are their role model. They follow your lead."

Kael's gaze cut to Liam's. "What?"

Liam heaved a breath. "You heard me."

Confusion morphed into outrage, and then into gut-deep guilt. Of course his warriors would follow his lead. Which meant that the decreasing population of their kind... was in part his own fault. Newlings couldn't be born without his warriors finding mates.

"It is time," Liam said. "Meara has been gone for three hundred years."

Outrage erupted in Kael's gut. No one said her name to him. *No one.*

But Liam pushed on. "She would want you to be happy. She would want you to have comfort. You know damn right well she would kick your ass if she knew how you denied yourself."

Kael braced his hands on his hips and hung his head. Well, that was true. Meara had been a fierce woman, full of life and laughter and aggressively loyal. And she'd believed in love. Kael would go as far as to say she'd taught him what love meant, why it should be valued.

"Jesus, Kael, if you've possibly found your mate, how can you even think of letting her go?"

Kael inhaled a shuddering breath and rubbed his lips with his hand.

Fuck. I let her go. No. I sent her away.

And now she was out there, somewhere. Unprotected. Vulnerable.

The Soul Eaters had found his clan's stronghold once. Though that particular band of evil had been eradicated, nothing said it couldn't happen again. Meara hadn't been his fault, he knew that in his heart of hearts. But if trouble befell Shayla after he'd thrown her out, that would lie at his feet.

And it would crush him. He would never, ever come back from it.

Icy cold panic sloshed in his gut, seized his spine. "Shit, Liam. I was horrible to her."

Liam stabbed him in the chest with his pointer finger. "Then make it right."

Kael nodded and massaged his forehead. Wanting her wasn't the question. Impossibly, he did, in every way and soul deep. But could he allow himself to be so vulnerable again? His heart panged and his hand dropped to his chest, then applied counterpressure to ease the awful tightness there.

Who was he kidding? Her loss already pained him. Resolve filled his gut and straightened his spine. "Get her," he whispered, his tone urgent and strained.

A smile full of boyish mischief and fraternal affection transformed Liam's face. "Right away, my lord, right away."

Kael glared and Liam straightened his face as he

sprinted from the room, but he moved with so much enthusiasm Kael couldn't resist the buoyancy of good humor that inflated his chest.

It constricted just as quickly. He needed to know she was safe. He needed to look into that mystical gaze. Anxiety tossed his stomach as he anticipated seeing her again. He couldn't imagine what she must think of him, how she must be feeling. Christ, she wasn't even down from the high of her orgasm when he threw her out.

Kael braced himself. Every likelihood existed she wouldn't want to return. And though that decision would level him, he wouldn't blame her one bit.

CHAPTER 5

VWK

If Shayla never saw a blindfold again, it would be too soon.

With her eyes covered to keep secret the rural location of the vampires' compound, she reclined against the leather of the luxury sedan's backseat. Having asked her trainer for some space, she rode alone. It was the middle of the night, just hours into the twentieth anniversary of her birth.

Happy freaking birthday to me.

She shifted and pulled her legs up under her on the seat. Unthinkingly, she rubbed her left hand, massaged her palm. At some point it had started aching, but she couldn't remember hurting herself. The gentle hum of road noise was soothing, at least. Anything to distract her from her thoughts.

The previous evening, the trip from Belfast had taken a little over an hour, so she knew it wouldn't be long until she was back at her hotel near the airport. She'd be returning to London tomorrow, and she could definitely get into the idea of losing an afternoon browsing the shelves of the Waterstone's at Piccadilly Circus.

Anything normal would be nice right about now.

The car slowed and veered to the left, and gravel crunched beneath the tires. Then they were still, only the soft purr of the idling engine filling her ears. The driver was separated from her by a privacy screen.

Shayla threw her hands out to brace herself as the car eased into what had to be a U-turn.

"Um, hello?" She reached forward until her hands found the facing seat and then shifted her body to reach the dividing window. She knocked. Nothing. "Oh, come on. Hello?" she called louder. She flopped back against the seat.

What is going on?

Maybe her trainer, a man she called Master Simon, needed a ride back with her after all. That must be it.

In the quiet lull of the resumed ride, all she could think about was how different the night had gone from what she'd expected. Yesterday, she'd been so excited, nearly giddy, as she imagined what the evening might hold for her. How meeting the king could very well be the answer to a variety of prayers.

Now, she was just depressed...and, frankly, a little annoyed.

Kael might be gorgeous and fascinating and sexy, able to make her come by kissing her alone, but he was just a...a *guy. For God's sake.*

Oh, who am I kidding?

Kael was everything she'd ever fantasized, and so much more. Powerful and magnificent in his otherworldliness. Gentle and kind, at least when he wanted to be. So damn hot her novice body and mind could barely process it.

He was also her best shot at getting justice for Dana and vengeance against the Soul Eaters.

Well, not anymore. Her years-long grief made her throat go tight. *I'm sorry, Dana. I'll find another way. I promise.*

Shayla hugged herself and laid her head back against the seat. She *would* find another way. Somehow. Some time.

As for Kael, well, the Proffered never had more than a few hours with him, did they?

Her rational mind knew that, expected it. Any hopes she held out otherwise were just the last hangings-on of teenage fantasies. Now she could put her daydreaming aside and focus on a realistic path to fighting the evil in her world.

If nothing else, there was her future role on the Electorate Council. Maybe she should talk to her parents to see if there was a way for her to participate sooner. Yeah, that was a starting place, at least. Surely there were also other contributions she could make she didn't yet know enough to conceive. That thought eased the tension from her neck and shoulders.

The car stopped again, pulling her out of her thoughts. She'd been so distracted she couldn't tell how much time had passed. Her door clicked open. From somewhere outside, voices bit back and forth at one another. She slid her blindfold off and set it on the seat beside her.

Shayla's eyes blinked and stung as they adjusted to the fluorescent lights of the cavernous garage—she'd guessed right, then, they'd returned. Through a squint, she was finally able to make out the shape of her trainer, a tall, thin man in his mid-forties, and—she was certain from his size and long braid—a vampire warrior. Chills raised the hair on her arms as she stepped out of the car.

Why was the warrior here if the point of her return was to collect Master Simon?

The men's conversation halted, and both turned to look at her. Their expressions were studies in opposites. Master Simon's entire face was frowning—it was his "concerned" expression, rather than his "angry" one, and she was a little relieved at that.

The big warrior, on the other hand, wore the most welcoming smile. He nodded once. "Hello."

His manner was open, friendly. It put her at ease, which was good since she had absolutely no idea what was going on. "Hey." She glanced at Master Simon, who was watching them, wary.

The vampire stepped forward and offered his hand. "I am Liam."

She looked at him for a minute, then placed her hand in his engulfing grip. "I'm Shayla."

He grinned as he shook her hand. "It's very nice to meet you, Shayla."

Shayla returned his smile, then bit her bottom lip. She was utterly confused and therefore had no idea what protocol was appropriate. She had a million questions, but no idea if she was free to voice them. A long moment passed with no one saying anything, unleashing a nervous energy inside her she could barely restrain.

Finally, she couldn't keep herself from breaking the silence. "Uh, so…"

"Come, Shayla. Let's talk." Her trainer held out his

hand in invitation and directed her back the way they'd come just an hour before.

She glanced between them for a minute and smiled wryly as Liam nodded encouragingly. She eyeballed the big guy, feeling a little wary herself now. "Yeah. Okay."

The three of them entered the reception area, passed through security, and threaded their way through several corporate-looking hallways until they returned to the posh apartment where she'd readied herself earlier.

Simon offered her a seat in the living area and she settled into an armchair and crossed her jeans-clad legs. A glass of orange juice and two of her favorite kind of chocolate-chip cookies sat on the side table. She managed a smile at Master Simon for his thoughtfulness and took a long sip of the cool sweetness.

The men chose seats around her. Master Simon and Liam traded looks, then Simon said, "The king would like to see you again."

Shayla nearly choked on a bite of cookie. The words were so far outside her expectations she merely blinked at them. Hope flared in her gut, but she tamped it down. Hard. No one saw him a second time. She tucked her long loose hair behind her ears.

Finally, she managed, "What? Why?"

Liam smiled and sat forward, but clamped his mouth shut when Simon glared at him. Her trainer's protectiveness warmed her heart. She'd always liked him, even when he was a pain in the ass. But he'd given her every confidence she'd be able to handle this night. She trusted him.

"He regrets what happened and would like to see you again," Simon replied.

Shayla pulled her eyes from Master Simon's guarded expression to Liam's eager face. The weight of what wasn't being said hung in the air between them.

The question was: did the why matter? If she put her hurt at Kael's earlier rejection aside, the answer should be no. Nothing had really changed. She'd committed to doing this,. Wanted to, even. And now she had the opportunity again.

This would truly be her last chance…for so many things.

"I see," she said as her brain analyzed what was really going on. She chanced another bite of the cookie, her thoughts reeling.

Liam's smile flagged a little as he watched her. His mood shift puzzled her. He seemed so invested in her decision.

She narrowed her gaze at him. "May I make a request? Uh, two, actually?"

"You may make them," Master Simon replied, "but I cannot guarantee to honor them."

Shayla had expected his response, but from the vampire's demeanor, she guessed she had a bit of negotiating power. She didn't understand why, but she planned to use it. "May I have an hour to prepare? I could use some time to…get my head screwed on straight again."

"That's an excellent idea, Shayla. Of course. And your second request?"

There was no way Simon was going to say yes to this one, but asking it couldn't hurt. "Well, um, may I have permission to, uh…ask the king a few questions?"

"No, Shayla—"

"Yes, definitely," Liam interrupted. He winked at her.

Master Simon gaped at Liam's outburst and Shayla

pressed her lips into a line to keep from laughing. She liked Liam, liked the feeling he was somehow her ally in…whatever this was.

Simon shook his head. "Yes, then, apparently. Does that mean you are willing?"

"Yes, Master Simon." Anticipation shot down her spine. She couldn't believe this was happening. Maybe she still had a shot, after all.

"Then, take your hour and be prepared for me at—" he looked down at his watch "—three-thirty? We will treat everything from then exactly the same."

CHAPTER 6

VWK

Kael stood on the hidden balcony carved into the basalt cliff face and soaked in the view of the crashing waves along the Antrim Coast. In the far distance, the volcanic formation known as the Giant's Causeway was just visible under the moonlight.

How many centuries had he admired the beauty of this harsh, unforgiving seascape? How many nights had he come here hoping the rhythmic motion of the sea would imbue him with the peace and tranquility that war and loss had leached from him so many lifetimes ago?

Footsteps approached from the stone corridor behind him. Kael braced against the thick ledge, expecting the worst. Deserving it.

"My lord?"

Tension drained from Kael's shoulders. Liam's voice told him the news was good. He breathed in the cleansing sea air and turned to his brother. "Thank you, old friend. She is well?"

Liam grinned. "She's great."

Kael's gaze cut to Liam's. "You spoke with her?" Liam nodded. "And what did you speak of?"

"Just introductions, really. Oh, and she wants to be able to ask you some questions."

Kael hitched an eyebrow. "Does she now? About what, exactly?"

The warrior scratched his chin. "Didn't say."

"And you didn't think to ask?" Kael's layered robes caught the wind and danced around his legs.

He shook his head and shrugged. "Figured it didn't really matter."

Kael nodded and ran a hand through the unbraided side of his hair. "Fair point." His mind raced as he tried to imagine what was going through *her* mind. What she might want to know.

He stepped toward the entryway and Liam moved to the side, allowing the king first passage. Liam secured the stone-faced door, constructed in such a way it was indistinguishable from the rest of the rock wall on the outside.

Anticipation lanced through him. "So, did she, uh, say anything about me, or, uh…" Kael pinched the bridge of his nose.

"Did she say anything about you?" He chuckled. "No, but I could pass her a note in study hall if you like."

Kael's fist connected with Liam's bicep before he'd really thought to do it. Damn, that little release of tension felt good.

Liam grabbed his arm and spit out an old Gaelic curse. His glare was indulgent, bordering on a smug smile. "Feel better, my lord?"

Kael clapped him on the back. "Much. Let's return to the chamber, shall we?"

Liam smirked. "She'll be up in about an hour."

Kael halted. "An hour?"

"She asked for some time."

Kael ignored the humor coloring his old friend's expression. "I guess I can't blame her." They resumed walking down the twisting passageway single file until it intersected with a main corridor. Liam secured a second door—this one modern, reinforced steel, before they continued on.

What the hell was he going to do with himself for another hour? As it was, he could barely restrain himself from showing up at the door to her apartment and begging her forgiveness. He shook his head at himself as they returned to the ceremonial anteroom to the feeding chamber.

"I don't suppose we need to replicate the cleansing ritual, do we?" Liam rocked on his heels as if he was the one eager for the next hour to speed by.

"I shouldn't think so." Kael braced his hands on his hips. "Then again, this is a bit irregular."

"Yes." Fraternal affection shone from Liam's eyes.

Kael turned away. Hope was the most dangerous of all the emotions. He would let Liam harbor enough of it for both of them, at least for now. Kael was trying hard to manage his expectations. Exactly how this would all work out remained to be seen.

And maybe it wouldn't work out at all.

Sighing, he walked to the feeding chamber door and opened it. He knew something he could do to pass the time. But when he looked to the floor by the far wall, the mess he'd created was gone. The tabletop stood empty, and the shattered glass, broken candlesticks, and crushed flower stems had been removed.

Kael turned to Liam, knowing without question he'd taken care of it. "Thank you, and sorry."

Liam waved him off.

A new idea flashed into mind, and it was brilliant. "Ah, I'll be back."

"My lord?"

"Ten minutes."

"My lord, this is highly unusual."

Kael's smile hurt his cheeks. "Yes, it certainly is."

"What if she returns before you do?"

Kael halted in the doorway to the antechamber. "Ah. Fair point. You wait here and tell her I'm sorry to keep her waiting but will only be a moment."

"*What?*"

"Thanks, Liam," Kael said, the rightness of his actions driving him away from the room. He marched through the empty halls to the small industrial kitchen. Although vampires could only consume the flesh of animals or liquids, particularly spirits, they kept other foodstuffs around for the few mated females, who retained most of their human physiology and still required regular nutrition, as well as for their human employees and the occasional human guest.

Whistling, Kael pulled open the refrigerator door, unsure what he might find. He didn't spend much time in this room. But he was determined to lay out an offering for her

One his own hands prepared.

A hearty sausage frittata sat on the center shelf. Perfect.

He pulled it out and placed two thick slices on a plate. A container of paper-thin prosciutto caught his eye. He retrieved it and some cut-up melon, and wrapped the ham around the juicy, orange chunks. His chef swore by the combination of the sweetness and saltiness, even if Kael couldn't enjoy the fruit. Next, he ladled marinated olives, artichoke hearts and red peppers from a covered dish into a bowl. It was likely he'd just raided the human staff's breakfast, but suspected he could find a way to make it up to them.

Kael cleaned up his mess and turned to the pantry. He added apples, oranges, and mixed nuts to the tray. The meal was turning into quite a feast, igniting a satisfied warmth in his gut. He yearned to see her nourished at his hand. He added a chilled bottle of water and a crystal goblet to the tray. He debated wine, but wanted them both clearheaded for the conversation he hoped they'd have.

As he wandered back through the halls, he whistled again as he juggled his load. Liam sprung from an armchair in the corner of the feeding room when Kael breezed in. The warrior's eyes went wide as he surveyed the contents of the weighted-down tray.

Kael settled the meal on the round table next to the bed, then poured the water into the glass. Satisfied, he turned and surveyed the room. The goblet of Shayla's blood and his dagger still sat on the stand across the room, and the blindfold and a single white flower lay on the floor.

They needed a clean slate. Those things had to go. He glanced at Liam. "I've got it from here."

"As you wish, my lord." Liam rose and made for the door.

"Brother?" Kael called out.

The warrior stopped with his hand on the knob and looked over his shoulder. "Yes?"

"I won't forget what you've done for me this night." Because Liam's words and actions—his willingness to fight with Kael—were quite possibly going to give him a second chance at life.

A *real* life. One with companionship and family and love.

Liam grinned. "Just don't fuck it up again." He winked. "My lord." He didn't even try to hide his smile as he left the room. The ornate door clicked behind him.

Kael chuffed out a laugh. And then there was nothing to do but wait.

He busied himself picking up and putting away the blindfold, cleaning and sheathing his dagger, and placing the small white flower on the edge of the plate of food. All of this allowed him to avoid deciding what to do with her blood. He hated to waste something so precious—precious not just because it was a virgin's blood, but because it was *her* blood. But if she rejected him, he wouldn't deserve it. And if she didn't, well…hopefully he'd never have to feed from a cup again.

He stared at the goblet a moment longer, then finally placed it on a shelf inside the large cabinet. His fangs stretched out in his mouth as the scent of it infused his consciousness. His throat burned and constricted as he secured the doors. Hunger clenched in his gut. Hunger for so much more than blood…

Before long, footsteps echoed in the exterior corridor and a knock sounded at the back door.

Kael swallowed hard and strode to the center of the room. "Come."

Simon Freneau pushed through the door and stopped on the threshold, bowing his head. "Good evening, Your Highness."

Kael stepped forward and offered his hand. "Simon. Good to see you again." The man nodded and shook Kael's hand, but his furrowed brow didn't speak of pleasure. Kael knew how protective the trainers were of the Proffered. He clearly had some amends to make. Kael's mistake, the failed hypnotism in particular, had made Simon look bad too. The women were told the pain of the whole experience was minimal to none, and that was true. Usually. "It won't happen again."

Not the least because he hoped to never again require the services of the Proffered. But that was up to Shayla—and the mating bond, though Kael swore the mystical connection of a blood match had been weaving its tendrils around him all night, drawing him to her. Body, mind and soul.

Simon nodded again and the muscles in his face relaxed, though he still didn't smile. "May I present to you the Proffered?"

"Please." Kael braced against the anticipation surging through him. He could smell Shayla, hear her small movements in the hallway.

Finally, she appeared in the doorway, a vision in a fresh white silk robe and styled mahogany hair. She stepped in and cleared the door, then took her standing position with her hands behind her back and her head bowed.

Simon looked between them once, leveled a pointed stare at Kael, and stepped backward through the door.

Shayla was counting her breaths again, trying to rein in her emotions, but his very presence was nearly undoing the past hour of relaxation she'd attempted. She'd started out with a quick yoga routine, stretching and working her muscles, then soaked in the tub. The concentration the braiding took also provided a great distraction, but it still seemed time had sped up when Master Simon knocked on her door.

Now that she was before Kael again, her neck and shoulders tightened as her apprehension increased.

"Shayla, look at me."

As much as she'd been waiting for his voice, it still startled her. His use of her name. His tender, regretful tone.

She knew she must obey, but was afraid if she did, she'd lose control of her emotions—and she wasn't sure whether hurt or anger would win out. Neither was appropriate to show, and both were likely to result in tears.

The king stepped toward her until he was easily within arm's reach. "Shayla," he whispered, coaxing her.

A long moment passed. And then he fell to his knees before her, his face tilted upward so their eyes could finally meet.

She gasped and her mouth dropped open. He was more fascinating, more gorgeous, than she had even fully recalled. Fire danced behind his eyes, and flashes of gold shined out through the emerald. He was smiling, and it highlighted the strong masculine angles of his jaw and cheeks so vividly it stole her breath. A reaction amplified by the appearance of the sharp tips of his fangs. Shayla licked her lips.

Despite being on his knees, he radiated such palpable power she could feel it jangling in the air between them.

Oh, God. He's on his knees.

A throaty sigh escaped her as she dropped to her own, head once again bowed. She was always to be below him.

"Now I can't see you again." The warm, amused tone was back. "Please look at me."

Taking a deep breath, Shayla finally obeyed. Her gaze raked over his intricate tartan robes before finally settling on his handsome face. When their eyes met, the smile he let loose dazzled her, luring her to smile back. His playfulness, the incredible sense of ease now possessing him, made it harder to hold on to her anger.

"Thank you," he said. She nodded. "I have some things I'd like to say to you. Are you willing to hear them?"

"Of course, Your Highness."

Kael frowned for a moment, and Shayla didn't have time to figure out why before he spoke again. "I hurt you, and I owe you an apology."

She inhaled to speak, but he cocked his eyebrow and she fell silent. She nodded again instead.

"I don't just mean for hurting you with the knife, although I am…beyond sorry you had to endure that." He grasped one of her hands in both of his and her lips fell open. His touch was so warm, so encompassing, so comforting, even though her one hand continued to ache. "I lost control and it compromised your safety, your well-being, and that is my first responsibility to the Proffered."

Shayla's shoulders and gaze dropped as he referred to her title again. She internally reprimanded herself for expecting anything else.

The fingers on his free hand nudged her chin up and beckoned her to look at him. "Shayla, I lost control because I...I felt something, with you. Something I don't feel...ever. I..."

She should've been focusing, listening, but... *Did he just say he felt something for me? With me? Lost control because he felt something...as in, he has feelings? For me?*

He chuckled. "Where did you go, young one?"

Shayla shook her head. "I'm sorry, Your Highness."

He squeezed her hand and dipped his head to look up into her once again diverted gaze. "Shayla, could you please call me Kael?"

Her eyes flew to his and she gaped. "Uh. Yes?"

His grin brightened his whole face. "Was that a question?"

"No, Sir—er, Kael." A blush bloomed hot on her face. It was a good thing she was on her knees, because the room began to spin.

"Mmm, that is lovely. And so fragrant." He fingered her cheek. "I would like to taste you, Shayla."

She gulped and shuddered as her heart took off at a mad gallop. Did that mean he would feed from her now? She didn't know. "O-okay" was all she could manage.

"Okay," he whispered as he leaned in slowly. So slowly. Her lips parted in needy anticipation. And then his mouth finally found hers.

This wasn't the wild kiss he'd claimed her with earlier. His lips claimed hers gently, reverently, as if he was savoring small tastes of a rare gourmet meal. One large hand grasped her shoulder and the other cupped her cheek—both brought her closer to him. He pulled and sucked at her lips, his hair falling around their faces as he rose up over her. She opened herself before he even demanded it of her—her body remembered his exquisite taste and begged for its return. Their tongues stroked and explored, but she needed more. She pushed forward just enough to suck his whole tongue deep into her mouth.

Sweet fulfillment exploded against her taste buds, dragging whimpers and moans from her. He groaned and her hands flew to his hair. Her left hand found masses of thick silky bronze she gripped and tugged as she held him to her, but her right hand fell on his jeweled braid. Knowing the significance of it, she yanked her hand back, afraid she'd offended him.

But then his big hand grasped hers where it rested against his chest and pulled it back up to his head. "Hold me," he whispered against her lips. "Touch me."

Shayla moaned her assent as her fingers wrapped around the braid and the jewels bit lightly into her skin.

Dear God she would hold him and touch him as much as he wanted. Now. Tonight. Tomorrow.

Forever.

Kael wanted to go slow. He wanted to seduce her—not just her body, but her heart, her mind. But his body was nearly vibrating with the difficulty of restraining himself. Her lust and adrenaline were heady scents in the air, but nothing compared to the tantalizing aroma of the sweetness of her arousal. Except maybe the deep sense of psychic calm that had invaded him since she'd returned.

His cock came to life, his fangs stretched out and rubbed dangerously against her tongue and lips.He pulled back. When he bit her this time, he didn't want it to be an accident.

"Can you forgive me, Shayla?" He searched her blue-green gaze. His life seemed to hang in the anticipation of her words.

She was breathing heavily and trembling. Her gaze was just as searching. "You hurt me."

Her words crushed him with guilt and enlivened him with pride in her for standing up for herself. The multiple sides of her personality fascinated him. She could be both submissive and fierce, obedient and challenging. And he adored that about her. "Yes."

She nailed him with a stare. "Not just with the knife."

A single nod. "I know. I'm sorry. I took my fear out on you. It was unfair and unkind. I truly regret it."

Shayla gave him an appraising look. Finally she sighed. "Don't do it again." The cocked brow above her blue eye enchanted him.

This wasn't a woman he could push around. This was a woman who would push back. He was thrilled. He bowed his head. "You have my word." She studied him, then nodded. He smiled. "Yes?"

"Yes," she whispered.

He grasped her cheeks and pressed his lips to hers. "Thank you." He tilted his head and kissed her right eye. "Thank you." Then her left. "Thank you."

She laughed as she fisted her hands in the thick folds of his robes. The delighted sound made his chest expand.

"My Shayla." *Ask her. Tell her.* Kael pulled back and licked his lips.

"What is it?" She reached a tentative hand up, her eyes asking permission. He nodded and her small, warm palm cupped his cheekbone, stroked his brow, tucked a thick strand of hair back off his face. Each gesture left him with the overwhelming feeling of being cared for.

It has been so long....

"I need you to understand me." He grasped her hand and kissed over her life and love lines. She tilted her head. "I want you."

"Good." She smiled. "You have me."

CHAPTER 7

S hayla meant those words down deep.
She'd fantasized about this man for years now. She'd had her first orgasms at the mere idea of him. Later orgasms had involved the only image she'd ever seen of him—a portrait in which the artist had well captured his powerful otherworldliness that attracted her so.

Not all her fantasies involving him had been sexual, either. She'd dreamed of fighting by his side, gutting a Soul Eater from navel to sternum and watching the life bleed out of its eyes. She knew that wasn't likely, of course. Though she was trained in martial arts and had taken shooting lessons, she knew enough to know she didn't have the expertise to be anything but liability in a real fight. But that didn't keep the violent images out of her secret imaginings.

Now that she'd met Kael, though, and felt the unbelievably intense pull to him, she knew her attraction was to more than just the *idea* of him, the *fantasy* of him.

It was to Kael, the man.

And he wanted her, too.

"You have me," she repeated, breathless as she watched his green eyes flare. "Have me."

Kael's mouth dropped open and Shayla gasped as she caught the white flash of a sharp tooth. She was darkly fascinated by this side of him and shivered at the thought that the man before her was not just a man, but a *vampire*.

Wanting him to know she was serious, she extended her wrist to him.

In one swift motion, he grasped it and pulled both of them to their feet. She gasped and fell into him. "Not. This. Time." His big hand cradled her face. "This time I want my mouth on you."

The words left her dizzy with want.

She followed him to the massive iron bed and watched, fascinated, as he unclasped his magnificent tartan robes. He still wore the thin green silk robe from before underneath, but she was distracted from thinking about that when he turned toward the bed and, in a graceful flick of his wrists, unfurled the layered tartans out over the bedding in a soft, gentle pillowing of fabric.

Shayla was glad he turned back to her so quickly. She wanted what was about to happen and her body ached for things she didn't even have the words to name, but if he gave her the chance to get nervous, to overthink it, she might.

He didn't give her the time.

Kael grasped her shoulders and pulled her against him, his mouth finding hers as if they'd never left off earlier. As her lips and tongue responded, he wrapped his arms around her. One large hand cradled her head while the other smoothed down over her back and settled just above her rear. The strength of his embrace pressed their bodies together. He was hard and thick and long between them. Need scorched through her veins. She writhed and pushed against him.

They kissed and explored each other until Kael was all that existed. His heat surrounded her. His male spice filled her nose and excited her palate. His touch, tender and possessive at the same time, set every nerve ending on fire.

He pulled away from her mouth and she gasped for breath, then moaned as he trailed openmouthed kisses and licks and long teasing drags of what had to be his fangs along her jaw and down her neck. He sucked on the pulse point below her ear. "I will take care of you, Shayla," he whispered. She shivered and tilted her neck for his exploration.

She cupped the back of his head as he leaned down to explore her body. The cool silk of her robe slid off her shoulders under the direction of his hands, then settled around her biceps like a shawl. He fumbled at her waist and the belt dropped, freeing the robe to swing open. Then he raked his gaze from her face to her legs.

His observation set off an electric current down her center. His lips glistened as he licked them.

When he met her eyes again, his were blazing. The brilliant green hue wavered and intensified. He yanked the tie to his own robe free and the fabric fell open, revealing a swath of muscular and marked male flesh from throat to groin.

An intricate black design pulled her attention from his face to the light golden skin of his chest. Mostly visible between the hanging green silk was a large round tattoo of a series of interlocking Celtic knots surrounding a regal Pict horse. The Celts' knot work represented the complexity of life, and the more overlapping the lines, the greater the protection against evil was supposed to be.

If the symbolism was true, Kael should've been well served by this beautiful mark.

Every inch of his body was lean golden muscle, much of it decorated by beautiful Celtic artwork. Every rippling of his shoulders and clenching of his defined abdomen radiated leashed power.

Finally, she couldn't resist looking at that most masculine part of him. Her eyes went wide and heat roared over her face. His shaft was thick and long, and hung heavily from the bronze curls covering his groin. She might have been a little scared if her core didn't clench in need and anticipation, if just looking at him didn't make her wet.

But it did. Holy hell, it did.

For long moments, she drank him in. When she noticed the faster rise and fall of his chest, she finally looked back to his face.

He was watching her observe him—his mouth hung open and his Adam's apple bobbed in a rough swallow. And his fangs, longer now, were completely visible to her for the first time.

It was like she'd never felt want before in her whole life. All she knew was that she needed him. In her. In any way. In every way.

A shiver ran through her, and she shifted her stance, adjusting to the moisture between her legs. She couldn't stand the distance between them and closed it with a sure step. With one hand against the horse tattoo on his bare chest, she reached up with the other and cupped the back of his head and pulled him down to her. She was stunned to feel a rhythmic beat under her hand and realized how much about him she wanted, *needed*, to know.

Later...

This time it was her mouth that claimed his. His fang pinched her lip and she moaned. Then she wrapped her tongue around the other fang and flicked it repeatedly.

His mouth tasted like danger and ecstasy.

Embracing his nonhuman side so wantonly felt decadent, but also like the most natural thing she'd ever done.

Kael fisted his hands in her hair but couldn't decide whether to pull her away or hold her there forever.

Definitely forever.

Now that he'd accepted the magic weaving around them, he felt it down deep. Being with Shayla this way was as right as breathing, as drinking blood. Her tongue curled around his right canine and he sucked in a breath and growled. His fangs were so fucking sensitive and her tongue was relentless. Pre-cum slicked the skin of her stomach where he thrust against her. She lifted a leg and wrapped it around his thigh. The sweet scent of her arousal exploded into his senses.

Called him home.

He groaned, then grabbed her shoulders and forced her backward until her body met the tall column of the iron poster on the bed. It took a little effort and even more resolve to release her from the kiss, to give up her stroking of his fangs.

But his patience was too damn close to running into the negative. And this time he wasn't chancing making a mistake.

Shayla gasped as her back bumped into the cold metal, which he imagined got colder as he pushed the robe the rest of the way off her arms.

"Arms up and grasp onto the post."

Breathing harder, she responded immediately and the pose perfected her posture and lifted her breasts.

"Yes. Yes, Shayla. Beautiful." He hummed in appreciation and pulled the belt off his robe, then shrugged out of it altogether.

Desire and need drew a low growl from his chest as he reached up with the silk tie. Seconds later her hands were secured to the bedpost above her head.

Kael ran his nose up her cheek to her ear and inhaled deeply. "I don't want to drink from you just yet—" He licked the shell of her ear "—so we're going to keep your hands up there where they won't be able to urge me to do something I'm not ready to do."

He nipped her earlobe and she rubbed her cheek against the scruff on his jaw. The intimacy of the small gesture tugged at something inside him, something that had been dormant for so damn long. He leaned back to find her gaze intense and aroused, her teeth biting her bottom lip.

He narrowed his eyes at the sight. "And so long as I can't bite you, no biting yourself." His thumb pulled the plump skin free of her teeth then rubbed across it. He couldn't begin to allow himself to imagine *her* doing the biting. "Fuck."

Now that she was so exposed to him, he took full advantage of what he wanted to do: worship her. Prove to her that he could be good to her and do right by her.

He started by caressing her breasts which he'd admired so greedily all night. They filled his hands with warm weight and he licked and kissed and suckled her pebbled nipples deep into his mouth. He worked back and forth between them, his fingers massaging and tugging the mound his lips weren't worshipping. She moaned and pushed herself further into his mouth and squeezed her thighs together.

Good. He wanted her as ravenous for him as he was for her.

Kael smiled at her squirming and dropped to his knees. Giving no warning, he pulled Shayla's legs out from under her and lifted them over his shoulders until her thighs rested on them. Her gasp of surprise morphed into a guttural cry when he anchored his mouth against her swollen, wet lips. He sucked and licked and penetrated her with his tongue. Her juices flooded his senses and coated his throat, taking the worst of the edge off his demanding thirst, but it wasn't enough.

It would never be enough, with her.

Shayla whimpered and pleaded between cries and moans. "Kael," she rasped, igniting a wave of his own pleasure at her free use of his name. "Ka—" His name trailed off into a throaty scream as her orgasm exploded around his mouth and radiated through the rest of her body in a series of muscle spasms. Her euphoria was magnificent.

"More, Shayla. Again." Making sure her sensitive flesh

was well coated with his soothing saliva, he nicked her swollen lip with his fang. She screamed and bucked when he surrounded the cut and her clit with his lips and sucked her flesh and blood over and over again.

Kael's body was in heaven and hell.

His cock swelled and leaked against his thighs. His sac, high and tight, ached for release. But her taste was so fucking rich and luscious—and, *Christ Almighty*, her blood was thick and warm and totally life-giving—he couldn't give any of it up without at least one more fast flow of her cream down his throat. And he wanted her delirious and boneless with pleasure.

Her keening and clenching muscles told him when she was on the verge. "No, no. I…I can't. No more. Mmm, Kael…oh, God, don't stop—"

Her babbling cut off abruptly as her orgasm stole her breath. Her thighs squeezed his face and her whole body thrashed. Kael supported her entire weight to insure the restraints didn't harm her wrists or shoulders. But her ecstasy was glorious and unleashed a raw feeling of masculine pride in his chest. He devoured every bit of her release, relished her sweet taste, her complete submission to his will.

And what he willed was her pleasure. Tonight. Forever.

When Shayla's body calmed, she sagged against him. Kael eased out from under her, rose and, with a quick flick of his wrist, removed the bonds. She collapsed into his arms, her movements so fluid someone seeing her might've thought her drunk.

"Shh, dearheart. I have you."

She nuzzled her face into the crook of his neck. Competing reactions erupted. The gesture was sweet and comforting, and tugged at his heart. But the proximity of her mouth to his throat also spiked his arousal as it conjured imaginings of her opening her mouth, drinking.

Taking him into her.

Sucking in a breath that failed to calm, Kael lifted Shayla into his arms and gently laid her atop his tartan robes on the bed.

And damn if she didn't look like that was right where she belonged.

Shayla blinked her eyes open and found herself sprawled out on the bed. Her arm brushed something soft and comfortable, and she recalled Kael spreading out his robes. She stretched and fought the urge to curl up and snuggle into them. His scent lingered all around her.

Kael.

She turned her head and found him. His hard body pressed against the length of her side. A light sheen of sweat covered his brow and his tongue dragged over his bottom lip like he was tasting her there. A passing thought urged embarrassment, but she was too blissed-out to feel anything but gratitude and contentment, especially when he looked at her with such hunger.

Teasing, dragging fingers caressed her from throat to pubis. His voice was rough, raspy, full of gravel. "Are you ready for more, Shayla? I don't mean to rush you, but I—"

She reached out and pressed three fingers against his full lips. "Don't even think of apologizing for needing me."

He hitched an eyebrow and kissed her fingers, then pulled them away. "Was that a command, milady?"

She blushed. "Take it how you will." She bit her bottom lip to restrain the smile threatening to erupt.

He growled. "What did I tell you about biting yourself?"

The animalistic sound, tension in his voice, and flashing gold behind his dilated eyes thrilled her and reawakened her body. "Well, someone ought to," she whispered.

It was quite possibly the most brazen thing she'd ever said. And she didn't regret it one bit. Not when his mouth dropped open and his fangs elongated. She squeaked as he easily pushed her further up on the bed and crawled between her thighs.

"Just someone, Shayla? Anyone?" He braced himself with one arm while his other hand rubbed the head of his cock through her slick folds.

The sensations left her dizzy and breathless. "You."

"Say it again," he growled. His muscles trembled and his eyes nearly glowed.

Her heart thundered against her breastbone, deep need making her crave his body in hers. She almost couldn't hold herself still the urge was so intense. "You. I'm yours."

"Your body?" He pushed the thick head of his cock into her wet pussy and stilled.

She groaned and looked down between them. The erotic vision of his shaft entering her body made her core clench. He bit out a curse in what sounded like ancient Gaelic. Her gaze flew to his. "My body is yours."

"Yes." He pushed in further and Shayla moaned at the incredible stretching and filling of the invasion. "Your blood? Who can claim your blood?"

Shayla found it difficult to speak through her panting. "Only…you."

His weight fell upon her and he braced himself on his elbows near her shoulders. One of his hands tangled in her braids and lifted her head up for a searing kiss. Finally he pulled away and trailed kisses to her ear. Under her hands, his taut muscles radiated leashed power. "Your virginity, Shayla, your womanhood," he rasped.

"Yours," she pleaded.

His body exploded in movement.

He thrust his hips until he was fully seated within her.

Shayla cried out, her body pulled between pleasure and pain. But he didn't give her time to feel the latter, because then he threw his head back, roared in a sound that could only be described as ecstatic triumph, and dropped his face to her throat.

He bit her, burying his fangs deep within the yielding flesh of her neck.

Shayla was overwhelmed, awash in competing sensations. The speed of Kael's actions surprised her and his pleasured shout drowned out her gasped whimper. His bite seared her throat. But all of that seemed as if in a different lifetime, because the very first sucking pull of his mouth against her throat removed every bit of pain from her body.

Euphoria. Complete and utter.

His movements possessed her, claimed her. He wrapped his body over hers as he hunched and thrust between her thighs. His hands cradled and held her as he moaned and sucked at her throat. Her body broke out in a sheen of sweat and she was slick everywhere, easing his way as he slid his massive taut frame above hers. She wrapped her arms around him and dug her fingers into his shoulder blades, his lats, his ass, as she tried to anchor herself to reality.

The suction at her throat pulled through her whole being until her toes curled against his calves. Surrendering entirely, her legs fell all the way open and she ground her center against his hammering thrusts. Each suck of his mouth throbbed in her pussy until she was mad with need.

Shayla whined and pleaded and nuzzled his hair and writhed beneath him. Kael growled as he fed and the sound vibrated through her chest.

Impossibly, her body detonated again.

She arched against his robes while her muscles clenched and pulsed around his length. For a split second, she went insane with the pleasure. Her mind couldn't handle it. The world disappeared in a floating blissful haze as she shuddered and moaned and gasped for oxygen.

It was glorious. And totally overwhelming.

Kael licked the wounds closed on her neck and looked down at her. "That's right, Shayla. So good. You are so fucking good."

Her heart swelled at his praise. She had nothing to compare him to, of course, but he was proving himself an amazing lover—passionate, attentive, and impossibly sexy.

She couldn't imagine needing—or wanting—anything more than him, than what he was giving her.

The fear of losing him at the end of the night burst into her brain and stole her breath for just a moment. It was true. It could happen. So she shoved the useless emotion away and focused on the incredible vampire still atop her. She wouldn't waste a moment worrying. She would burn every touch, every sensation into her memory.

In case that's all she had come morning.

Satiation surged through Kael's system. Her powerful blood fed his muscles and reinforced his humanity. Shayla was magnificent beyond his hopes and expectations. Her body was decadence personified. Her eyes blazed with life and acceptance. Her hands held and touched him and made him *feel*.

And her words, the longing and…*familiarity* with which she called out his name.

It was their first time together, but it felt as natural as if they had always been.

Her orgasm all played out, Kael withdrew from her and sat back on his haunches. He pulled her into a sitting position and kissed her, long, languid twists of lips and tongues that spoke of much, much more than lust.

Shayla's hand curled around his still-hard cock, her grip tentative at first, and then surer, harder. Kael gasped, and their gazes collided.

"You haven't…" She looked down to where she stroked him.

He shook his head. "I'm not done with you yet, Shayla."

Her eyes widened as her cheeks pinked. Her heartbeat tripped into a sprint loud enough for him to hear and pronounced enough to cause a vein to jump at her throat. "I see."

"Do you now?" That vein had him licking his lips. "Turn around," he whispered against her mouth as he leaned in for a deep, lingering kiss. "I want to watch you as I claim you."

Trembling, Shayla moved until her back was to him. He pressed a large hand against her spine and she fell forward onto her hands and knees.

"It's so much deeper this way. And I want every inch of you."

He pushed home and they both groaned. He went slow, tormenting them both with his restraint. When he'd first entered her, Kael the Fair had disappeared in favor of a nearly feral vampire who craved blood and carnal pleasure in equal amounts. That raw male remained in him, just under the surface. But Kael wanted to draw this out, wanted to revel in every sweet sensation. It had been so long since sex had been about more than just slaking a physical thirst.

Wrapping his arms around her abdomen, Kael pulled Shayla into a kneeling position over his lap. Every bit of his skin screamed for contact with hers, and this way he could hold her as he took her.

And there was another benefit as well. He cupped her chin and guided her eyes across the room to where their movements were reflected in a huge gilded mirror hanging on the wall.

"Watch," he commanded.

With one hand, Kael fondled and teased Shayla's full breasts. Using his other hand and his massive thighs, he set a hot, satisfying pace gliding in and out of her velvety heat and chasing what he knew was going to be massive orgasm, one that hopefully delivered a revelation that would change the rest of his life.

Shayla urged him on with her searching hands, first

gripping his hips, then reaching back over her shoulders and tangling in his hair. She murmured a string of whispered encouragements full of belonging.

The energy in Kael's body congregated in his groin, tightening his muscles and stealing his breath. "Shayla," he panted as he thrust and observed the beauty of their joint movements, "I want you. I *want* you."

It was a chant, a prayer, a plea to the fates.

"Yes." Her hand fisted in his hair and she reclined her head and kissed his cheek. "I…want you…too."

"Please," he cried, begging her, imploring the ancient blood magic that joined mates together. Unable to wait a moment longer, he sank his aching fangs into the yielding flesh of her throat.

His body was wound so tight from the intensity of the whole night with her, this time the first hot pull of her life-giving fluids unleashed his orgasm. He clamped down tighter—his mouth on her neck and his arms around her body—as he bucked against her. His cock pulsed again and again, releasing his seed deep within her. He devoured her blood, unable to stop sucking but knowing he needed to. She would already be drained from her earlier blood loss and the sheer vigor of their lovemaking.

Finally, he eased his fangs from her neck and licked her wound, his body still shuddering Around him, the room seemed to spin. He anchored himself to Shayla, held her close and prayed.

As the last streams of his cum filled her, Kael felt it: a sharp tingling radiating out of their still-connected loins, up his chest, and down his arm to his right hand. He gritted his teeth against the biting burn and squeezed Shayla in reassurance when she cried out at the sensation.

"It's okay, dearhreart," he managed. "It's okay."

Her head went slack against his shoulder and she unleashed a deep, sleepy sigh. He tilted his gaze to the ceiling and whispered strained, fervent words of gratitude in the ancient language.

He laid her down on the bed and stretched out alongside her. She immediately turned her body toward his. Their gazes met for a brief moment. The corner of her lip raised in a half smile. And then she fell asleep.

Lifting his hand, Kael admired the intricate mating mark, a series of symbolic knots that wrapped around the front and back of his hand. He was amazed by it, in awe. His heart ached with fullness and hope. Long-lost joy flooded his mind, enlivened his soul. Joy not just for the chance at a mate again, but because it was her.

Shayla.

Her beauty and grace and strength had already breached his heart.

He fingered the unique pattern, different from the one he'd shared with Meara. Its disappearance from his skin upon her death had been salt in the devastating wound of her loss. Never again. His life would be first and foremost about protecting Shayla's.

Assuming…

He shook his head and focused on the decadent sight of her luscious curves, curled up against him, so trusting and vulnerable in her repose. He wished she would awaken so they could join hands and see the way the marks flowed from his right to her left in a continuous, conjoining pattern.

But as her heart settled into a normal pace again, he resolved to let her rest and recuperate.

Hopefully, there was no rush. They would have all the time in the world.

As long as she wanted him the way he wanted her.

Completely. Totally. Forever.

CHAPTER 8

VWK

Shayla was deliciously dazed, sated like she could never need anything again in her whole life. She stretched against the soft covers and her muscles ached in a way that reminded her how she and Kael had used one another so thoroughly. She rubbed her eyes, trying to remove the grogginess from her head.

Unexpected color caught her attention and she stilled.

Beautiful, thin black knots covered her left hand.

She gasped and bolted upright.

Kael appeared out of nowhere, wearing the emerald silk robe again, and settled on the bed beside her. He placed a tray near her knees and held out a glass of water which she gladly accepted, nearly draining the entire thing as if she'd been lost in the desert. She lowered the glass against her leg and raised her hand, then looked at Kael.

He grasped her left hand with his right and kissed it. Her eyes drifted to his mirror markings and she gaped. The hair rose on her arms and neck. "What…?"

Kael shifted onto his knees on the bed. "Shayla McKinnon, this mark proves what I already suspected. You are my mate. You are destined to walk beside me, rule with me, share my blood and, through that, my immortality."

"Mate?" Shayla's mind raced as she traced the incredible marking with her fingers, then followed her tracings onto his hand. "What...I mean, I don't..."

"I know, dearheart." He kissed her forehead and sighed. "Just relax for a moment. We have time to talk." He folded a length of tartan over her legs and waist and scooted the tray closer to her. "You must be hungry, yes? I brought you some food. I know it's not much, but..." He shrugged.

She tugged the robe up to cover her breasts and glanced at his face, found him a little shy for the first time. "I'm starving, actually, and this looks and smells delicious." She picked up some cashews and popped them in her mouth, all of a sudden ravenous for the feast before her. "Thank you."

His smile was dazzling, proud, and grew as she polished off her piece of the savory frittata and, at his insistence, half of his, the spicy olives and artichokes, most of the nuts, and an orange. Her mind raced with questions and buzzed in amazement, but she was so ravenous it was as if she couldn't think about anything else until that hunger was finally sated.

"I feel like I haven't eaten in days, and this was fabulous." With a satisfied groan, she pushed the tray away. Kael's eyes flared at the sound, which unleashed a new hunger low in her belly.

How could she want him again so soon? But she was suddenly insatiable for more than just food...

Kael inhaled deeply and chuckled, ran his hand through his hair. "I like the way you think, Shayla, but perhaps we should talk first?"

For a split second, his words confounded her, but then he took another slow, deep breath in through his nose and licked his lips. Could he…? Oh, jeez. He could! He could smell her. She crossed her legs where they were extended in front of her.

Kael frowned and gently encouraged her ankles to part. "Never feel bad for wanting me," he said, echoing her earlier words in a low, serious voice that amped up her desire further. "Because you can be sure I'm always hungry for you."

Shayla shook her head, blushing and smiling as his expression softened into something she would've sworn could only be described as adoring. She drew her legs up to her chest and embraced them, rested her head on her knees so she could see him.

"So, talking then…" She admired the design on her hand. Realized the ache she'd earlier felt was gone. She gasped. "Is this why my hand has felt so odd all night?"

An oath in that strange language spilled from his lips, low and fervent. "You felt it, too?"

The awe she felt was reflected back to her in his green eyes. "Yes, but what does it mean?"

"That this…that *we* would make a very strong mating."

She looked at the swirl of knots on her hand again. "Mating," she whispered, trying out the word.

"Yes. Oh, Shayla. This pleases me. Greatly. I want you to know that. I hope it pleases you, too." He tucked his right hand into her grip, once again joining their marked hands.

She thought of all she'd hoped for from this night. "It does, Kael, more than you know." She squeezed his hand.

"But how does all this work? What does it mean practically? For me and for us?"

He tilted his head. "*More than I know?* Tell me what it is I don't know, then. Please?"

She nodded. "I will. I promise. But please explain all this first. I need to understand."

He stretched forward and kissed her cheek. "Of course. In my world, Shayla, blood is magical, powerful, the source of all life. Some blood, when joined together, is especially strong, especially right. For a vampire, that rightness can manifest in a bond that identifies mates who would be a good match, who would bear strong offspring. And it is a rare, special thing."

Shayla studied her hand, his words opening up new worlds in front of her, worlds she'd only dreamed of and never once thought would truly exist for her. "So, we're mated now?" A cacophony of reactions flooded her mind.

Awe. Joy. Triumph. All awash in a sensation of utter surrealism.

Kael's eyes flared. "No. Not yet. The mating mark lasts for three days. If the mating ritual isn't completed within that time, the mark will disappear along with the chance to ever be together. If you agree, on the other hand, there will be a ritual ceremony to affirm the bonding and celebrate the start of our life together, with you as my queen, sharing my world, my blood, my immortality."

She frowned and struggled to make sense of her thoughts.

Queen? Immortal?

So, getting what she'd always wanted came along with some things she hadn't imagined. Did that really matter? "I see," she said as her mind worked, compiling pro and con and to-do lists, weighing options, and imagining alternate paths. She knew she couldn't accept the mating without some sacrifice on her part. She was twenty years old with a world of opportunity and possibility in front of her.

But then she looked at Kael and realized that everything that had ever motivated and interested her, everything she'd ever imagined would make life worth living, was sitting right next to her on the bed.

She could have eternity to ask him her questions about his life and times.

She could have justice for Dana. Vengeance against the Soul Eaters.

She had to tell him. "Before, when I said there were things you didn't know?" He nodded. "When I was fourteen, my older sister was murdered by vampires."

Kael gasped and moved closer, one arm threading around her shoulders. That preternatural light flared in his eyes, but it was darker somehow, more menacing. "Soul Eaters," he growled.

"Yes. Before they drained every drop of blood from her body, they raped her. Then, when she was dead, they slit her open and ripped out her heart. That was how she was found. Those are the images my parents have to carry around in their heads." Shayla held her breath and refused to surrender to tears and grief.

"Were you close with her?"

She smiled and released her breath. "Yeah. I mean, you know, we drove each other crazy like siblings do. But she was my hero. She'd just graduated high school…" She shrugged and braced herself internally against the rush of old but ever-present pain. "What happened to her, well, I have to play a role in bringing justice to the animals that did that. I've never known what that role would be, exactly, just that I *had* to do something. What do you think of that?"

He studied her for a long moment, then leaned forward and dragged his nose along the skin of her arm. Pressed a kiss there. "Many years ago, I was mated, and she conceived a child."

"Yes," Shayla whispered, reaching out and trailing her fingers through his hair. She'd learned Kael's history, of course, it was part of why she imagined he might understand what drove her, but hearing it from the man himself was something else all together.

"When Meara was in her fourth month, the Soul Eaters attacked Dunluce. We'd been betrayed by one of our own whose treachery went as far as allowing them entry to the castle, and we were caught completely off guard. The assault began at four in the morning when they used our own cannon against us to destroy the walls, insuring there would be no protection from the sun when it rose. Meara shepherded the women and children to the relative safety of the dungeons. There is no telling how many lives she saved. But she went into labor. It was too early and she was bleeding. I was above, engaged in the fight, pinned down and outnumbered when my blood felt her alarm. By the time I could get to her, it was too late. The newling was gone and she'd hemorrhaged so badly feeding her could not save her."

"I'm so sorry," Shayla said. Could she ever replace such a woman?

He turned his face and kissed her hand where it was still stroking him. "Thank you, but that is not why I told you about her. You asked what I thought of your need to act on behalf of your sister."

Shayla nodded, a little scared of what he might say next.

His gaze met hers and held nothing back. "I understand it, completely."

Kael's words stole the breath from Shayla's throat and wrapped themselves around an old, damaged part of her soul.

He wasn't only her dream. He was her dream come true.

She threw off the covering of his robe, embraced his big shoulders and climbed into his lap, straddling him. She swallowed his groan as her center ground against his cock, already waking under her. The kiss was intense and sensual, full of compassion and shared grief and understanding.

Kael pulled back and rested his forehead against the bridge of her nose. Then he met her gaze again. "*You* must understand, though, my dearest heart," he began in a strained voice. "I could never expose you to the kind of danger that took Meara from me. My intention would never be to stifle your dreams or impose my will as if…"

She lifted an eyebrow. "As if you were my king?"

One side of his full lips quirked up. "Is it wrong that I like the sound of that?"

The heat of a blush warmed Shayla's cheeks. Truth be told, she did, too. "No, as long as you don't think it's going to get you your way in everything."

"Sometimes, though?" His fingers made slow, teasing drags up and down her spine, igniting delicious shivers and chills.

She grinned. "Maybe."

"Maybe." He threw his head back and laughed, and Shayla loved the sound of it, loved that she'd been the one to make him laugh. After a moment, his expression grew serious again. "I only mean to say, I understand your need, Shayla, but I could never tolerate you out there…exposed… fighting." He grimaced at the words. "My warriors are many, strong, well-trained. They will fight for you. As will I."

His words were a promise, fierce and true and utterly male. She knew he was right about the fighting, but her heart ached at the idea there wasn't *something* she could do. "I know, but, isn't there anything, anything at all—"

"Of course there is." He crushed a lingering kiss against her mouth. "You can stand by me, and give me the strength to face the fight. You can advise me—I'll never hide from you the difficulties we face. You can facilitate our relationship with the Electorate Council, and secure the alliance between vampires and humans. You can feed me, and make me strong. And in turn, my warriors will feed more frequently, as they must, as they should've been doing all along. You can bear our children, and bring new warriors into the fight."

So much passion imbued his words they brought tears to Shayla's eyes. He made her believe she really could make a difference.

For Dana. For herself. For him.

"Oh, Kael."

"And, another thing, I spoke with Simon while you were asleep. I wanted to assure him of your well-being, well, after earlier." The lightest of blushes colored his cheeks. He shook his head. "I have learned you are quite a scholar, Shayla, of the history, culture, and languages of the British Isles, of the Celtic people in particular."

She was almost embarrassed at the pride filling his voice. She hugged herself and nodded. "Yes. Though, how would mating impact my ability to finish my degree? Would I have to give it up?" The thought made her stomach flip-flop. On the one hand, he personally embodied the very history and culture that had fascinated her all these years. On the other, her twenty-first-century mindset balked at giving up her education and career to marry and have babies. Not that she didn't want those things, for she truly did. And Kael's words only bolstered that desire.

"Simon suggested the reminder of your studies might be doable through telecourses. We have archival collections and rare books here you could use for your research. Maybe you could even impose some order on our library, insure the records of my people are known among us and well preserved. And—" he twisted his lips and looked down "—we could send security along with you on any trips you might *have* to make to complete your degree."

She wouldn't have to give it up?

Would long-distance course work even be possible? Would her program allow it? And, what might be in his records, documents surely no one had ever studied before? Questions fired through her brain and energized her with the idea there might be a way to have both, do both.

"Kael. Thank you. Even if that can't work out, just the fact you inquired about it, entertained the possibility." She grasped the skin over her heart. "It means so much."

"I'm pleased you are happy." He tucked a thick strand

of hair behind her ear, the gesture so full of caring. "So, does this mean…"

Only one other concern held her back from an enthusiastic acceptance.

He said the mating bond pleased him, but would it ever be more than that? Would he ever love her? Could she ever replace the love he must've felt for Meara?

A warm fullness in her chest told her she was falling for him, maybe had fallen for him already—after all, she'd had years of imagining them together. Having met him, she now knew that his beauty, his gentleness, his fierceness, his playfulness, his power—they comprised the real man, not just fantasy. But she wanted him to want her for her, to *ask* her to be his. She rubbed her hands together and studied the stunning, intricate markings.

She wanted it to be more than just some…mystical… biology that drew them together.

Kael let out a deep sigh and gently moved her off his lap. He rose and cleared the tray from the bed. Then he turned to her. "This is a lot to take in. And I'm sure the pressure of the deadline is difficult. I will prepare an apartment for you. Anything you need will be provided—"

"Wait. What? Why?" She scooted herself until she was sitting on the edge. Though she was entirely comfortable being nude in front of him, the air was chilly against her tired body. She pulled the robes up over her lap again and tucked them under her arms to cover her chest.

"I need you to be close until you've made your decision. I cannot send the woman who may be my mate out into the world unprotected. But I don't wish to pressure you any more than necessary, so I will give you your own—"

"I can't be with you?" Shayla didn't know the protocol. No part of her training had covered *this* amazing possibility. But didn't the mark mean they were to be together?

Kael's mouth dropped open and his eyes flared. His cock stirred the silk of his robe "What are you asking, Shayla?"

She shook her head and pushed off the bed, then situated the robes around her shoulders. Kael hummed at the sight and the sound connected with every nerve in her body. "I guess—" she inhaled a bolstering breath "—well, I'm… not asking anything."

"I do not understand." He cupped her face in his hands. "Please, dearheart, do not torment me."

Shayla smiled and held up her hand. "Is this just… chemistry? Biology?"

Kael frowned down at the pattern on his palm, then looked back to her eyes. He studied her for a long moment, then sank down to one knee and grasped her marked hand in his.

"Our mating is chemistry and biology. My body, my blood, needs you on a fundamental level. *You*. Your body brings me peace, comfort. Your blood restores my immortality and humanity. But I wanted you before this, Shayla. I brought you back because I knew, even then." He held their joined hands to his heart. "You are more beautiful than my eyes can take in. Your eyes enchant me and hold me to you. You are brave and fierce and strong and bright and these are just the things I've learned in the few hours we've been able to share. I want to know more."

Shayla bit down on her lip, trying to restrain the tears and joyous sob that threatened. Kael reached up and pulled her lip from her teeth with his thumb. He arched an eyebrow and she couldn't hold in the laugh-cry that escaped.

"Be mine, love. Please."

Love. Her heart exploded in her chest. "Yours? Forever?"

His smile was beatific. "If we're lucky."

She closed her eyes against his magnificent image and breathed deeply. Life flowed through her, and she knew at once it had led her to this moment, this man, this love.

"Yes, Kael. My answer is yes."

CHAPTER 9

K ael paced his sleeping chamber, his bare feet sinking into the plush emerald carpet...

He smiled.

That was where the differences with the previous night ended. He could hardly believe only twenty-four hours had passed since he'd walked the length of this room cursing the Night of the Proffering.

Tonight, it was nerves that had him wearing a path into the thick pile. He and Shayla would be mated this night, in a little less than an hour. Anticipation threatened to explode him apart.

"Just an observation, my lord, but you have a big night ahead of you. Keep pacing like that and you're likely to wear yourself out."

Kael halted and whirled on Liam, arms crossed and leaning against the wall by the door. The warrior's smirk was good-natured, and Kael chuckled and shook his head. He'd nearly forgotten Liam's presence in wondering what Shayla would look like. But as his second in command, he'd helped the king ready his clothing and adorn his body for the ritual. His garments all shared the deep crimson and gold of his clan crest, though the red was more significant for its reference to the blood that would bind him and Shayla together. The leather hugged his thighs, tormenting his already sensitive body. He couldn't don the cloak, though, until the blood marking his skin fully dried.

In front of a mirror, Kael carefully fingered the red smears coloring the knot over his heart. He twisted his torso to see the marks on his arm and back, too.

Liam appeared in the mirror behind him. "Dry?"

Kael nodded, simply mesmerized by a sight he thought he'd never see again—the ancient symbols for fidelity, fertility, protection and eternity painted over his skin in his own royal blood.

They would serve as Shayla's first tastes of him and fuel the blood hunger her mating mark would already have unleashed within her. A growl rumbled low in his chest at the thought.

Liam laid a hand on his shoulder, careful to avoid any of the marks, and squeezed. "I believe it is time, my brother. You don't want to be late to your own mating."

Kael nodded, emotion tightening his throat. He turned and faced Liam, whose eyes were alive with happiness and pride. "Thank you, old friend."

"You deserve this, Kael. It has been far too long since I've last felt joy flowing through your blood. I am honored to stand up for you this night."

Unable to respond, Kael clasped his grip around Liam's forearm, who returned the ancient warrior handshake. "You are a good man, Liam."

"Come. Let me help you with the cloak." He released Kael's arm and gestured to the bed.

Kael turned away and awaited the heavy fabric to fall upon his shoulders. Warmth surrounded him. He slipped his arms into the long, loose sleeves. The fine velvet was soft and thick, of the same deep crimson as his pants. Using the mirror again, Kael fastened the three ornate gold clips that held the cloak together over his chest.

Liam crossed the room to Kael's dressing table, and eased open the lid on an antique carved wooden box sitting there. Liam lifted the crown, encrusted with the same jewels Kael wore in his hair, and returned to stand before him.

"Your crown, Your Highness." Liam bowed his head and held the golden circle up in both hands.

Like the blood adorning his body, Kael had not expected to wear one of these again. As the sovereign, he had several crowns for different occasions. This mating crown had been made new, completed just a few hours before by the Warrior Ronan, who was also a skilled goldsmith. Kael settled the metal atop his head and adjusted it. "The hood, please," Kael managed in a raspy voice.

"Yes." Liam lifted the wide hood over Kael's head, careful not to snag the pointed ornaments on his headdress or the jewels in his braid.

Now he was ready.

Together, the men made their way through the manor house to an older part of the underground compound. Once again, the halls were empty and candlelit. It seemed to take forever to arrive at their destination, but finally Liam was opening the arched doors to the Hall of the Chieftains, where the mating ritual took place for all who lived herein.

All eyes turned to Kael as he entered the room. Six clan warriors formed a circle around the center of the room, each standing at a marked symbol tiled into the floor—symbols that represented elements of the heraldic badge of Clan MacQuillan. The vampires present were his senior clan warriors, his oldest compatriots, the closest thing he had to a blood family. Indeed, he was tied to each of them by a blood connection.

Kael watched as Liam crossed to the far side of the room and disappeared through a similarly arched door.

Then Kael took his place at the center of the circle, dropped to one knee, and waited.

"I do believe it is time for you to be mated," Ciara announced.

Shayla nodded and accepted the woman's hand. With assistance, she rose from the seat in front of the ornate vanity where she had been readied for the ceremony. Nervous energy gripped her, but so too did something else. An urge she'd never before felt, and somehow knew would only be eased by Kael's presence, flowed through her, held her muscles taut, resonated in an empty ache in her gut. She clenched and released her left hand.

"Thank you," she said, smiling at Ciara and Maeve.

The women had spent the day with her while the men assisted Kael, or at least that's what she'd been told. Ciara and Maeve were warriors' mates and great sources of information and reassurance for Shayla. Ciara was the mate of a warrior named Marcas, and though she appeared Shayla's age, she'd been born in 1922. Even more stunning was Maeve, who was mated to Ronan and had been alive for three hundred years.

Shayla had taken an immediate liking to both of them. They'd helped prepare her for the mating ritual and surrounded her with friendship and sisterhood, easing the pang in her heart that no one from her family could share in the ceremony. Kael had explained the previous night that they would be notified and invited for a special wedding dinner soon.

She was the only human who could attend the mating ritual.

Ciara helped her put on the velvet cloak over the rich silk gown she wore. With its plunging V neck and thin lace straps, it was more lingerie than gown, but it was gorgeous, bejeweled with glittering beads along the neckline, empire waist and bottom hem.

"Lower your head," Maeve said. Shayla stooped down and bowed her head. Maeve and Ciara lifted the cloak's hood over the bridal circlet, careful not to muss the intricate braiding and bejeweling of her hair.

"Now, remember," Ciara said with warm smile, "that should be the last time you bow your head to anyone, save your king. In an hour's time, you will be queen."

The very idea made Shayla's head spin. Flustered, she tried to speak but no words came out. She didn't know what to say. All three women fell together, laughing.

Finally, she calmed herself. "Well, my new friends, my future husband does not strike me as the most patient man. So, should we go?"

Ciara and Maeve led her through stone hallways

where priceless art decorated the walls and sat atop pedestals. But Shayla's need to see Kael was intense and she could not pay the pieces the attention they deserved. Forever seemed to pass in the time it took to arrive at the arched wooden door of the room they'd shown her earlier in the day.

The Hall of the Chieftains.

Liam waited next to the door and offered her a warm smile when their eyes met.

"Liam will take you from here," Ciara said, her expression affectionate.

Shayla nodded at her new friend and exchanged hugs with both women before they departed.

Liam turned to her and held out his left arm. "It would be my honor to escort you to your mate."

Trembling, not out of fear but out of an urgency she could not fully explain, Shayla grasped Liam's forearm with her unmarked hand. He opened the door and guided her forward.

In an instant, Shayla's gaze fell on Kael's kneeling form and he was all she could see.

The desire to run to him made it feel as if her insides were vibrating. She licked her lips and released a shaky breath. Her left hand tingled and she fisted against the maddening, arousing sensation.

Kael's eyes glowed the brightest she'd ever seen. He was magnificent, regal, and more beautiful than she'd remembered after just a day's painful separation. A fierce masculinity rolled off him and curled around her until she swore she could smell him, taste him, feel his touch on her skin.

Liam paused at the outside of the circle and dropped his arm.

And then Shayla stood before the man, the vampire, the king she knew without question owned her, heart and body.

They joined marked hands and she barely resisted crying out. She sucked in a sharp breath as the most wondrous current of belonging shot through her—she simply didn't know how else to describe it. By the trembling of his hand in hers, she knew Kael felt it, too.

On instinct, she sank to her knees. They were so close her chest nearly touched his. Only their clasped hands separated them.

Then Kael began to speak. She didn't know the ancient language, but she understood perfectly well the emotion behind the words. Her heart swelled at the passion with which he spoke. Tears bloomed in her eyes at the glassiness she saw in his. Their hands clutched tighter and the feeling was simply, fundamentally right.

She was so focused on Kael she didn't even react when he paused and the warriors chanted in a fierce yell and fell to one knee around them.

After a moment, Kael's deep, fervent voice continued. "I am on my knees before you because we will always be equals, partners in all things. I hold your hand in mine, because we will always be together. I look into your eyes to see into the real you, and let you see into the real me. I pledge to take care of you, protect you, and cherish you for all time." Shayla's heart thundered in her chest. A single tear quietly rolled down her cheek. He raised their hands to his mouth and kissed her fingers.

Her lips dropped open and her mouth salivated at the

picture of his mouth tasting her. That foreign urge flared within her, stronger now, more demanding.

"The ancient blood magic has deemed us a good match. I agree with all my heart. Shayla McKinnon, will you be my mate?"

She swallowed hard and smiled. "Kael the Fair, Son of Iain, Warrior King of the Vampires and Chieftain of Clan MacQuillan, I will be your mate. I, in turn, pledge to take care of you, protect you, and cherish you for all time."

Intense heat flared between their palms, stung and burned, and then the pain disappeared completely. Kael flipped their hands over and pulled his wrist back enough to reveal new identical knot-shaped marks covering their palms. Unlike the rest of the mating mark, the knot was colored in greens and reds and blues. It was stunning.

Another roaring cheer rose up around them. The warriors bowed their heads.

Shayla was overwhelmed as her whole world changed around her, but above it all was her need for him. For Kael. She was dying to kiss him. It was almost painful to keep her mouth away. She bit down on her lip, hard, and chewed. With her eyes, she pleaded with him.

His gaze narrowed. "I understand, dearheart. Soon."

She undid the fastenings on her robe as he undid his. She exaggerated the lift of her hood, not wanting to catch the jewels in the circlet of her hair. Kael did the same, revealing a magnificent crown that made her hands itch with a need to bury themselves in his glorious hair. They both dropped their cloaks behind them.

Then Shayla gasped. Her gaze trailed down to the golden skin of his chest, painted with red markings. She breathed deeply and exhaled a needy moan she couldn't restrain. "My lord?" she whimpered, completely overwhelmed by his scent. It was him, only magnified by a million, and it drove her crazy. She shook and panted, was on the verge of begging for…she didn't know.

"What do you want to do, Shayla? What urge are you fighting? Give in to it."

Her gaze cut from the red to his flaring eyes.

"Give in. Do it. Now."

CHAPTER 10

Shayla licked her lips as she gazed at the red-painted knot over Kael's heart. She wanted to…to…

She sprang at him and opened her mouth over the red. The moment her tongue touched his skin, she groaned, a nearly strangled sound from deep in her throat. This was the urge she'd been feeling all day. She licked and sucked at the spot over his heart until only his clean tattoo remained. She drew back, whimpering.

Not enough. It wasn't enough.

"Here," he rasped. He pointed to another symbol painted on the bulge of his bicep.

Needy sounds spilled from her as she pulled his arm to her mouth. She feasted on the mark, but it, too, was gone too soon.

He held his hair away from the left side of his throat. "Again."

She moaned and climbed up him. His other arm strapped her against him, held her in place while she sucked and licked the red away. Kael grunted and shook under her frenzied attention and it drove her on.

It was blood. His blood. It sang to her, beckoned her.

She needed more. So much more.

Kael couldn't decide which ached worse, his throbbing fangs, elongated in preparation for the blood exchange, or his cock, which had hardened when Shayla walked into the room and approximated something like steel the moment her eyes discovered his blood.

She was so magnificent in her bloodlust that he reveled in every wanton lick and rough suck of her mouth on his skin. Her need and enthusiasm was more than he had hoped, and so sexy he feared he wouldn't be able to restrain himself from burying his shaft in the wet heat he could already smell right here in the Great Hall.

There were too many eyes here for that, though.

The witnesses were there to affirm the worthiness of the chosen, testify to the strength of the blood match and communicate to the human mate her acceptance into their community. In his case, the warriors' presence also assured the acceptance of whatever newling heirs he and Shayla might have—having witnessed the match, his brethren would be able to defend the child's birthright if ever challenged. Beyond what was required for the ceremony, though, Kael would never share her naked body with another male, not even just to watch.

The very thought made him prone to violence.

Shayla whimpered and panted against Kael's left ear. "More? Please?"

"My back," he said, his voice a raw scrape.

She spun around him and pressed up tight against him as she feasted on the large mark that spanned his shoulder blades. Her arms wrapped around him and her fingernails dug into his chest muscles.

Nearly three hundred years had passed since a female had fed from his veins, since he'd had the deep satisfaction of nourishing a woman from the fruit of his body. His soul nearly sang for the return of such raw, primal pleasure.

Shayla's arms circled his throat. "Oh, my God, Kael, what's happening to me? I…I…"

"One more, Shayla. You're doing so well." He hauled her body around his and laid her head in his lap. He took a deep breath that failed to calm, then stuck his thumb under the buttons of his leathers and pulled down, opening his fly on one side to expose the flat expanse of his lower abdominals.

Fingernails dug into his clothed ass as her mouth latched onto the fertility symbol. She sucked so hard he was sure she would leave a bruise, and he relished the idea of her marking his body, claiming him in every and any physical way.

She whined, and he knew the blood was gone. Triumph surged through him.

Nearly frantic to have her, he threaded his hands under her arms and drew them both into a standing position. She swayed at the sudden movement, but he easily steadied her. For the first time, he had a full view of the incredible silk gown that skimmed over her luscious feminine curves. Her eyes refocused and raked his flesh, and he felt it as an almost physical caress.

It was time.

He was so hungry for companionship. For love. He had no doubts now, none at all, about what he felt for the woman before him.

Kael reached up to his crown and grasped the central ornamental spike. Pushing a concealed release on the back, it clicked free and became the handle to a small hidden dagger. Shayla gasped when she saw it, then her face went pale when he placed the glinting blade to the taut base of his neck and sliced into his carotid artery.

Blood flowed freely in a dark, pulsing stream over his collarbone to his sternum.

And Kael just smiled.

Shayla's thoughts had completely devolved to animalistic urges and she reveled in it. The heady spice of his blood—its taste and scent—unleashed an erotic euphoria within her that she didn't think she would ever be able to give up or live without.

So as the thick red spilled down his chest, Shayla's whole body ached to have it.

Her gaze flashed from the blood to Kael's face, and what she saw there lanced heat and need through her body—pride, encouragement, desire.

He gave her a single nod.

She hesitated only a second more before gripping the corded muscles of his lats and curling her tongue around the heavy bead of blood running downward. The life-giving nectar exploded in her mouth, tasted about a thousand times more powerful directly from the source.

The source.

Her gaze fixed on the wound. Licking fast and greedily up his chest, Shayla arrived at his collarbone, swallowed the savory fluid coating her mouth, and latched her lips and teeth around the cut.

Shayla was utterly unprepared for the ecstasy of drinking directly from him. On the first full pull of his blood, she came so hard she went blind for the full duration of her orgasm. Brilliant light filled her entire visual field as every nerve and muscle in her body seized and jerked. Her juices trickled from her and slicked up her thighs.

Kael's tight embrace supported her and he cried out a victorious roar that echoed through the hall.

Her entire physiology seemed to explode and remake itself as his blood completed the alterations she now knew the mating mark had begun. Almost instantly, she felt lighter, healthier, stronger, invincible.

And then his fangs punctured the tender spot at the base of her throat, and Kael began to feed from her as she fed from him.

An approving shout rose up from the surrounding men at his actions.

Her embrace with Kael was every bit as intimate as having sex. Maybe more. Because blood was central to sustaining his life…

And, now, hers too.

She drank and drank until she felt glutinous, but could not pull herself away. He devoured her in the same uncontrolled, needful way, setting off a deep satisfaction within her chest, between her legs. The longer it went on, the more attuned to the blood's movement she became, and she realized they were literally exchanging blood.

She flowed into him. He flowed into her.

Her heart felt as if it might rupture. Surely, such a small organ could not contain emotions this intense.

I love him. Oh, God, I truly love him. Kael. My Kael.

As I love you, my dearest heart.

His voice in her head startled her so much she nearly released her suction from his neck. His hand tangled in her hair and held her down, petted her, encouraged her to take all she wanted.

Do not fear, Shayla. We are a part of one another now, inside each other. Our blood connection creates a telepathy that is strongest when we feed and make love.

Shayla was in awe of the rightness of his voice in her mind, like he had always been there, providing solace, comfort, companionship. But, just in that moment, there was something else she desperately needed.

I need all of you in me, Kael. Please. I'll go crazy if I can't have you.

A possessive growl rumbled against her breasts. *We are fully mated, love. I wait only for you to be sated before taking you back to our chamber and making love to you until the sun rises. Over and over again. Until neither of us can move a muscle.*

She moaned against his neck. *Just a little bit more. I just…* She rushed and gulped at the life-giving sustenance.

We have all the time in the world. Slow down. Take your time, dearheart. Savor. Remember? Never apologize for needing me.

After a few more minutes passed, Shayla's thirst was

finally quenched. Slowly, she released her mouth from his neck, shocked to see the deep impressions of her teeth marks in an angry circle.

She gasped. *Oh God, I'm sorry.*

For what? For being enthusiastic? For being a little rough? My fangs are still buried an inch into your flesh, yes? Teeth marks come with the territory. A warm chuckle accompanied the thoughts. *I know what I said, Shayla, but I need just a bit more of you. You taste so good, I don't want to stop.*

Whatever you want, whatever you need, it's yours, Kael.

She stroked his hair and held him, adoring that he needed her as much as she did him. Her earlier urgency subsided, though it didn't disappear altogether. Deep down, under her skin, a low-level need remained, maybe would always remain.

She hoped so. She never wanted to lose this feeling.

Free from her earlier bloodlust, Shayla became aware again of the men surrounding them, heads bowed and eyes averted, but still witnessing their union. The embarrassment or self-consciousness she might've expected never came. Her conviction in the rightness of all she had shared with Kael made it impossible to feel anything but confidence and pride and love.

Kael released her flesh and licked the wound closed. Because of his body's natural healing powers, his cut had already knitted together.

He threaded his fingers into her hair and ran maddening openmouthed kisses from her chest, up her throat and over her chin. Finally, he claimed her mouth, tenderly, reverently. Minutes passed, or hours, she couldn't really tell, before he broke off the kiss. Their marked hands joined, Kael pulled Shayla to his side.

The warriors formed a line before them with Liam at its center. The fierce masculine approval they each wore made her feel like she was one of them.

"My brethren, I present to you my mate, our queen, Her Majesty Shayla MacQuillan," Kael said in a strained, proud voice.

All of the warriors lowered to one knee in a coordinated movement, bowed their heads, and declared in one voice, "Your Majesty, we are at your service, now and forever."

Tears pricked Shayla's eyes and words spilled from her lips before she'd thought what to say. "As I am at yours, and our king's."

Approving murmurs and nods moved through the men.

"Rise now, brothers, and be merry."

The group surrounded them, clasped arms with Kael and offered him their wishes. To her, they bowed and complimented the match. A deep sense of family and community embraced Shayla, and she knew this was where she belonged.

But, just then, her interest didn't lie in bonding with the warriors assembled around them, great as they seemed to be.

She wanted Kael.

The floor dropped away from her feet as he swept her into his arms. He winked and pressed a kiss to her forehead.

The men laughed and applauded.

"Well, my friends, if you'll excuse me. I would like to have my mate to myself for a while." A crooked grin brightened his face. "A long while." He backed toward the door, still carrying her. "You see, I, too, plan to be in the service of the queen."

Shayla gasped at his brazenness but couldn't help her laughter, especially once the warriors started throwing catcalls at their retreating forms.

Good humor radiated from her lover, and his pleasure lit up her insides in return.

Kael paused outside a room she'd never entered. "Our private apartment," he explained as he carried her over the threshold. He kicked the door closed behind them.

She could live on the adoration she saw in his eyes. *"Mo chuisle mo chroí,"* he murmured. *You are the pulse of my heart*, she heard in her mind.

"I love you, Kael." She pressed a lingering kiss to his full lips.

"I love you, too," he murmured around the edge of the kiss. "So much."

She pulled away and rested her forehead on his, looked deep into his eyes. "I meant what I said in there, my love. I will always be in your service."

"We are partners, now, Shayla. Equals. We will be in one another's service, in all things."

"I love the sound of that."

"Mmm, so do I." He turned on his heel and crossed the large living room. "And I suggest we begin right now."

Shayla laughed as he picked up speed and pushed through a door into a large bedroom. In the center of the space sat a king-size poster bed with layers of gauzy, sheer panels hanging down from the four corners. That was all she had time to notice before Kael threw her onto the bed and sprawled on top of her.

His kisses started soft, but quickly became demanding, needy. She felt his urgency and returned it. They kissed and shared whispered declarations of love and removed each other's clothing until nothing in the world stood between them.

Everything she'd ever wanted she held within her arms and the cradle of her thighs. Her Vampire Warrior King. Her Kael.

Then he was in her once more.

And they well served each other all that night. With love and passion. Over and over again.

※

Thank you for reading! I hope you loved meeting Kael and Shayla. The next book in the Vampire Warrior Kings series is SEDUCED BY THE VAMPIRE KING. Find out what happens when exchange student Kate runs from her fate—right into the arms of an injured vampire who takes her prisoner. Need another reason to grab the next book? I have four words for you: Hot jail sex scene.

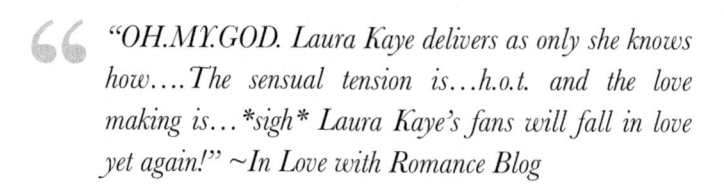

> *"OH.MY.GOD. Laura Kaye delivers as only she knows how....The sensual tension is...h.o.t. and the love making is...*sigh* Laura Kaye's fans will fall in love yet again!" ~In Love with Romance Blog*

※

Reviews are so helpful to authors and other readers. Please leave reviews of this book on Goodreads and your preferred retailers' sites. Thank you!

Read on for an excerpt from SEDUCED BY THE VAMPIRE KING

READ THE NEXT BOOK IN THE SERIES!

SEDUCED BY THE VAMPIRE KING
CHAPTER 1

Nikolai Vasilyev was right in the middle of the shit, and it was exactly where he wanted to be.

Shots erupted from two positions ahead of him and ricocheted off the abandoned cinder-block streetscape he'd been patrolling. Ducking into an alley, he felt a telltale whiz of air buzzing his ear and went flat against the concrete wall of the old factory. The frigid winter night air burned Nikolai's lungs. His hackles rose and his fangs stretched out. His enemies were close enough he could feel their evil.

He wanted trouble. And he found it. Or it found him. Semantics.

Somewhere ahead, concealed among the long-neglected buildings, a band of Soul Eaters apparently had a sniper's roost. Those demented murderers jeopardized the hidden vampire world by caving in to the lure of exsanguination. All vampires drank from humans, but only the Soul Eaters consumed human souls by drinking through the last beat of their hearts, then removing and eating it. Their addictive recklessness threatened to expose them all to the broader human world, and escalated the ancient war between the two rival strains of immortals.

Nikolai plotted out a plan of attack, the street taking shape in his mind's eye like a 3-D simulator. Dark satisfaction pooled in his gut. Sending these little birdies flying from their nest—permanently—was going to turn this night from a miserable waste to decently tolerable. It didn't get any better than that for him.

Not anymore.

Not since he'd dishonored himself, and the Soul Eaters killed Evgeny and Kyril.

The hushed, efficient chatter of his warriors sounded in his earpiece and drew Nikolai from his thoughts. Torturing himself over his brothers' deaths had no place out on the street. There was plenty of time for that while the sun kept him inside cooling his heels.

He peeked over his shoulder and around the corner of the building. A volley of shots rang out and Nikolai growled a curse under his breath, his gaze swinging around to the rusted industrial street lamp illuminating his position. He sighted the bulb and squeezed off a single bullet that solved that problem, then turned, fell to a crouch and took another light out farther down the street.

"Who's got a lock on that gunfire?" came Mikhail's voice through the earbud. His second-in-command was a consummate soldier and the only thing holding his kingdom together at the moment. Nikolai was man enough to admit that. "Report in."

One by one, six of his finest warriors gave the all clear and confirmed their locations.

Nikolai sighed. He didn't want to share this one. He didn't want to have to rein himself in. When he found the Soul Eaters' position, he wanted to unleash the inhuman monster within, to surrender to the grief and rage boiling inside him as he tore his enemies to pieces with his bare hands and fangs. No fucking audience required.

As if they all didn't worry about him enough. He hated the weighted silences and sidelong glances that seemed to follow him wherever he went these days. Christ, he needed to release a little of the volcanic agony expanding in his chest, making it hard to breathe, hard to think. Hard to care.

An awkward silence passed before he heard, "My lord, what's your area of operation?" Mikhail's tone no doubt sounded level and professional to everyone else, but Nikolai recognized the wariness and exhaustion in his oldest friend's voice. Guilt soured his gut. "I say again, my lord, what's your AO?"

Focusing on the task at hand, and not the way he was failing Mikhail—hell, failing all of them—Nikolai did a quick ammunition check and ran through his mental plan one more time. He took a deep calming breath and centered himself, using his memory of the last time he saw his brothers, expressions frozen in death, to fuel his resolve.

"Son of a bitch, Nikolai, answer me. You're there, aren't you?"

With indecipherable words still ranting from the

speaker, Nikolai tugged the unit from his ear and yanked it from around his neck. He dropped it to the ground and crushed the receiver with his boot, insuring no one could come behind him and eavesdrop on his warriors' movements.

With an apology to Mikhail and a vow to Evgeny and Kyril, Nikolai moved out onto the street, staying low and tight to the building. He set his sights on the general location from which the earlier shots seemed to originate and ducked into doorways and alleys whenever he could. Twenty meters ahead, a third street lamp posed an insurmountable problem. Whether he got rid of it or left it intact, he would reveal his position to the enemy.

He voted for the cover of darkness and took it out with a single shot, only the sudden blackness and sprinkling of glass against the concrete sidewalk revealing what he'd done.

It was enough.

A barrage of gunfire erupted, the snaps and crackles of high-speed projectiles close enough to make him dive for cover. The enemy fire brought something useful with it, too —the Soul Eaters' muzzle flashes gave away their position and told Nikolai precisely where he needed to go.

Release and relief were so fucking close.

The break in the gunfire meant they'd likely lost his position in the dark, so he bolted from his place behind a car and flashed across the street at preternatural speed. Closer now. He was so close he could smell their fear. He reveled in it. Drank it down into his belly like the sweetest nectar. Soon, he would gorge himself on it.

Reconnoitering the new side of the street, Nikolai shoved out of his hiding place and darted across the intersection to the block that housed the Soul Eaters' fortified position.

Victory lured him forward, out into the open.

Bullets rained down around him, but he ducked and twisted, plowing onward. His fangs pinched his bottom lip as he hauled ass to safety. A doorway loomed ahead, one that should be shielded from the nest above.

A new barrage of gunfire clattered and echoed in the space between the wasted buildings. The sound hurt his head and disoriented him. Nikolai couldn't place its location.

And then searing fire tore into his shoulder, the side of his neck, the back of his thigh.

Fuck, somehow they'd gotten behind him. And no one was covering his six.

Because he hadn't let them.

He was hit. Hit bad.

Howling more from the agony of defeat than the pain of the tainted bullets, poisoned with the blood of the dead, Nikolai flashed down the side street before the blood loss and infection drained his powers, his life. He pushed himself to keeping moving and lost track of the distance he covered as he retreated from the abandoned industrial quarter toward the general direction of Moscow's city center.

His breathing was loud in his own ears, a mix of a rasp and a gurgle that told him the neck wound was critical.

Son of a bitch. Mikhail was going to kill him. Assuming he survived.

The poison hit his heart as the industrial area gave way to apartment buildings and shops. He crashed against the brick wall of a building and his vision blurred and twisted.

READ THE NEXT BOOK IN THE SERIES!

The world went sideways and he hit the ground so hard it rattled his brain in his skull. Between the blood loss and the poison, moving took herculean effort, but he had to get off the street.

Gun still tight in his grip, he dragged himself on his forearms, pulling the dead weight of his body toward a gravel path that ran alongside the building. His muscles screamed, sweat stung his eyes, and his gasping breath scorched his throat. A thirst more intense than any he'd ever felt made his tongue feel thick and his fangs ache.

As the building's shadow covered him, Nikolai could move no more. He hoped the kingdom he'd refused to lead these long months would survive the succession crisis his death would leave behind.

Regrets. Oh, so many regrets.

Bitter cold bent his bones until he was sure they would snap. He shivered, sending his teeth and fangs clattering against one another.

How wonderful it would be to have the warmth and companionship of a mate right now.

He had not strength enough to even chide himself for the thought.

A black fog descended, stealing first his sight, then his hearing. Tortured thoughts remained to the end until, mercifully, they too faded to nothing.

Just like him.

Order SEDUCED BY THE VAMPIRE KING Today!

ABOUT THE AUTHOR

Laura Kaye is the New York Times and USA Today best-selling author of over forty books in contemporary and erotic romance and romantic suspense. Laura grew up amidst family lore involving angels, ghosts, and evil-eye curses, cementing her life-long fascination with storytelling and the supernatural. Laura lives in Maryland with her husband and two daughters, and appreciates her view of the Chesapeake Bay every day.

Visit Laura Kaye at LauraKayeAuthor.com

Subscribe to Laura's Newsletter:
http://smarturl.it/subscribeLauraKaye

facebook.com/laurakayewrites
twitter.com/laurakayeauthor
instagram.com/laurakayeauthor

ALSO BY LAURA KAYE

Vampire Warrior Kings Series
IN THE SERVICE OF THE KING
SEDUCED BY THE VAMPIRE KING
TAKEN BY THE VAMPIRE KING

Want more vampires?
FOREVER FREED

Hard Ink Series
HARD AS IT GETS
HARD AS YOU CAN
HARD TO HOLD ON TO
HARD TO COME BY
HARD TO BE GOOD
HARD TO LET GO
HARD AS STEEL
HARD EVER AFTER
HARD TO SERVE

Warrior Fight Club Series
FIGHTING FOR EVERYTHING
FIGHTING FOR WHAT'S HIS
WORTH FIGHTING FOR
FIGHTING THE FIRE – COMING 2020

Blasphemy Series
HARD TO SERVE
BOUND TO SUBMIT
MASTERING HER SENSES
EYES ON YOU
THEIRS TO TAKE
ON HIS KNEES
SWITCHING FOR HER – COMING 2020

Raven Riders
RIDE HARD
RIDE ROUGH
RIDE WILD
RIDE DIRTY
RIDE DEEP – COMING 2020

Hearts in Darkness Duet
HEARTS IN DARKNESS
LOVE IN THE LIGHT

Heroes Series

HER FORBIDDEN HERO
ONE NIGHT WITH A HERO

Stand Alone Titles

DARE TO RESIST

JUST GOTTA SAY

Printed in Great Britain
by Amazon